"Have some fun and loosen up a little."

Abby shimmied her shoulders side to side for emphasis.

"I'm loose." Clay shook his own shoulders.

"Prove it!" she yelled above the music.

She threw herself into Clay's arms, and he spun her around on stage feeling freer than he had in years. Her face was inches from his and her lips parted when their eyes met. He closed his for a moment and that was all it took for Clay to forget where they were...

His lips crashed down on hers, pent-up frustration colliding with his desire for the one woman who had turned his head for the first time in years.

When he finally heard the whoops and howls from the crowd, he released her. Abby stared up at him for a moment before hopping off the stage, leaving Clay to stand in the spotlight alone.

Dear Reader,

Sometimes ideas for books come from the craziest of places. *A Texan for Hire* came about when I was flipping through a Yankee Candle catalog. One of the scented pages instantly transported me to Ramblewood, Texas, and there stood Clay Tanner and Abby Winchester. I saw them so vividly that I stayed up all night outlining the first draft of this book. Subsequently, when I purchased my Mini Cooper shortly thereafter, I named it Abby—and when you read this book, you'll understand why. While Clay and Abby weren't originally part of the Ramblewood series, Clay's story was too important not to have a book of his own, and Abby's arrival in town will uncover almost three decades of secrets. Ramblewood will never be the same.

I'd like to thank David Canton from *My Texas P.I.* for his willingness to educate me on the ins and outs of private investigating. His advice was invaluable.

Feel free to stop in and visit me at amandarenee.com. I'd love to hear from you. Happy reading!

Amanda Renee

A TEXAN FOR HIRE

AMANDA RENEE

HARLEQUIN® AMERICAN ROMANCE®

Recycling programs
for this product may
not exist in your area.

ISBN-13: 978-0-373-75561-5

A Texan for Hire

Copyright © 2015 by Amanda Renee

Printed in U.S.A.

www.Harlequin.com

Amanda Renee was raised in the northeast and now wriggles her toes in the warm sand of coastal South Carolina. She was discovered through Harlequin's So You Think You Can Write contest and began writing for the American Romance line. When not creating stories about love, laughter and things that go bump in the night, she enjoys the company of her schnoodle, Duffy, photography, playing guitar and anything involving horses. You can visit her at amandarenee.com.

Books by Amanda Renee

HARLEQUIN AMERICAN ROMANCE

Welcome to Ramblewood

Betting on Texas

Home to the Cowboy

Blame It on the Rodeo

Visit the Author Profile page
at Harlequin.com for more titles

For Duffy...you define unconditional love.

Chapter One

Abby Winchester wasn't used to waking up in a strange bed, let alone one in a strange town, thirteen hundred miles from home. Mazie's Bed & Biscuit in Ramblewood, Texas, was a far cry from her early nineteenth-century row house in Charleston, South Carolina.

She sat up and yawned, replaying the events of the past month in her head. Abby's world had been turned upside down. It had begun with the death of Walter Davidson, her biological father, and had ended with the hospital board once again turning down her animal-assisted therapy proposal. As a physical therapist, Abby was determined to increase her patients' rehabilitation options, and despite the hospital's latest rejection, she vowed to continue fighting for the program she so passionately believed in.

And she would have focused on a new course of action if it weren't for one thing...the note the nurse had given her after Walter died. Scrawled in his handwriting on a piece of scrap paper were three words:

FIND YOUR SISTER.

Only one problem...Abby didn't have a sister. Well, not one she knew of.

Even though Abby doubted the rationality of Walter's

dying words, they continued to haunt her. With no other clues to go on, she had decided to begin her search in Ramblewood, the town of her birth. After she'd driven halfway across the country in one straight shot, she was exhausted.

Abby squinted at the nightstand clock—half the morning was already gone. She forced her road-weary body out of bed, breathing deeply as her feet hit the floor. Fortunately the moving-car sensation that usually followed an extensive road trip had subsided.

Her dog, Duffy, lifted his head as Abby stood. She scratched him behind his ears then padded to the bathroom. The knobs on the freestanding vintage faucet above the claw-foot tub creaked as she turned them. It was well after midnight when she'd arrived and she'd been too tired to summon the strength to take a shower. Abby would be forever grateful that the inn's owner, Mazie Lawson, had checked her in so late. Abby wouldn't have been able to handle one more minute cooped up in her car.

Feeling more human after she had bathed and dressed, Abby made her way downstairs with Duffy in tow. She chose an apple-pecan muffin from the basket on the dining room sideboard as her beloved sidekick tugged her in the direction of the front door.

Once outside, they headed for the Ramblewood Bark Park. Located next door to Mazie's Bed & Biscuit, the animal-friendly play area was an added bonus for guests of the converted Victorian inn, which catered to people traveling with their pets.

Duffy tugged on his leash as they walked through the park's double gates. Her schnoodle couldn't wait to run with the other dogs. Some would call her schnauzer and poodle mix a mutt, but Abby referred to him as her designer dog. Once they were securely inside, Duffy sped off to explore his new surroundings.

The pond in the middle of the park enticed panting canines to take a refreshing dip. Some dogs stood belly high, enjoying the coolness of the water—but not Duffy. He didn't have a particular fondness for anything wet, more like a distinct hatred. He tolerated a bath. Barely. There'd be no convincing him a swim was a good thing.

Abby smiled as she watched Duffy make friends with a cute female Scottish terrier. If dogs could talk, she was pretty sure Duffy approved of this trip.

She sat on a wooden bench under a tree, perusing emails on her phone while her dog played. A slight breeze rustled the maple leaves above her head. The early September air was still heavy with Southern heat. However, the temperature didn't bother her— One-hundred-degree days weighed down with one-hundred-percent humidity was the norm for summer in Charleston. The air in the South Carolina peninsula between the Ashley and Cooper rivers was thick with moisture most of the year. Ramblewood's dry weather was a welcome relief. She looked up at the sound of Duffy's barking. He barreled at her like a bull out of a chute. A black standard poodle was hot on his doggy heels. Duffy darted under Abby's bench, pivoted and then shot underneath the poodle. The other dog scrambled to keep up.

"Is the little silver bullet yours?" An older woman with closely cropped, curly salt-and-pepper hair asked as she approached. The dogs had reached the other side of the park before Abby could finish nodding.

"Barney won't hurt him," the woman said. "He loves to run."

"Oh, I'm not worried," Abby said. "Duffy loves to be chased. I swear he thrives on it."

"I can see that." The woman laughed, joining Abby on the bench. "I'm Kay Langtry, by the way."

"Abby Winchester," she replied, shaking the woman's hand. "You have a gorgeous dog."

"Thank you. He's quite a handful. Thirteen months and getting into everything. Barney's new trick is counter surfing, and he's tall enough to reach even the things I've pushed way to the back. I bring him out here to run in a more confined area because he wreaks havoc at the ranch—even the horses keep their distance."

"I can imagine." Abby watched Duffy and Barney run along the outskirts of the park. Her dog was fearless when it came to other dogs, but she could see he was keeping a safe distance from the pond. He refused to get his feet wet.

"Are you visiting someone in town?" Kay asked.

"Is it that obvious?" Abby glanced down at her jeans and T-shirt. She had thought her clothes were Texas appropriate when she threw them on earlier. Maybe she should've chosen a less bedazzled pair, but all of her jeans were heavily embellished with sequins and rhinestones. Now they seemed like overkill for the laid-back town. "I live in Charleston, South Carolina—originally from Pennsylvania—and I'm here on business. I'm staying next door at the Bed and Biscuit."

"How long are you in town for?" Kay asked.

"Not sure. A week at least, two at the most." Abby debated telling the woman her reasons for coming to Ramblewood. What harm would it do? Besides, the more people who knew her story, the more they might be able to help in her search. "I'm looking for my long-lost sister."

"I love reunion stories." Kay clasped her hands in her lap. "When did you two last see each other?"

"Never. My biological father recently died and left

me a note telling me to find my sister. I didn't know I had one up until that point. I thought I'd start here since I was born in Ramblewood. I'm banking on someone remembering my parents."

"What are their names?" Kay asked.

"Walter and Maeve Davidson. They divorced when I was a year old and my mom remarried a year later."

Kay listened intently. "Your story is better than an episode of General Hospital!" The woman's eyes widened. "Your parents' names don't ring a bell. Have you considered hiring a private investigator?"

"Not really." Abby didn't want to admit she'd spontaneously hopped in her car and headed west on a whim. Walter's note had troubled her more than she'd openly admitted. "I arrived in the middle of the night, and I'm not exactly sure where to start. I thought I'd stop by the courthouse first, but maybe an investigator isn't such a bad idea, providing it doesn't cost me a fortune. Do you know of anyone local?"

"It just so happens that I do, and I think you'll find him to your liking." A broad smile spread across Kay's face as she removed a cell phone from her bag. "Clay Tanner. That boy practically grew up in my house alongside my four sons. I guess I shouldn't call him or any of them boys anymore. But no matter how old they get, I still picture them running around my house laughing and full of mischief. He's single, to boot."

"Single, huh?" Abby laughed. "Kay, I'm looking for my sister, not a man."

"I don't see a ring on your finger, so I'd say you're free to explore the possibilities of what Ramblewood has to offer."

Abby had never seen a person's eyes twinkle before, but she could have sworn Kay's had done just that. The woman jotted Clay's number on the back of a crumpled envelope she found in her purse and handed it to Abby.

"I wish you the best of luck and if I can be of any help, feel free to give me a call." She pointed to the paper. "I wrote my number on there, too. I own the Bridle Dance Ranch and you're welcome there anytime. Ask anyone in town and they'll point you in the right direction." Kay checked her watch. "Speaking of such, I need to head home and figure out what I'm going to serve my growing brood for lunch. You'd think once they married and moved out of the house, they'd be able to feed themselves. Instead I have double, sometimes triple, the number to feed."

Kay rose from the bench, put two fingers to her mouth and performed a screeching whistle. Barney immediately stopped and changed direction, leaving Duffy behind. "It was a pleasure meeting you, Abby."

"Same here." Abby stood, and looked at the phone number in her hand. She was on a mission to find her sister. If this Clay person could help, then why not call him right away?

Her hands trembled as she entered the numbers into her phone. Sure, she wanted answers, but this man might actually find them. Up until last week, Abby had fought with herself and her family over the possibility that a sister might exist. She had figured Walter would have told her sooner if it were true, or at the very least, made it part of one of the birthday scavenger hunts he sent her on each year.

Since her parents' divorce, Abby recalled seeing Walter maybe four or five times in her life. He had moved to the West Coast when she was still in grade school. After Abby's brother, Wyatt, had been born, she hadn't understood why her last name was different from the rest of the family's. Her stepfather had offered to adopt her. Walter hadn't put up a fight.

Almost ten years ago, on Abby's eighteenth birthday, Walter had contacted her. He'd explained why he had walked away. He hadn't wanted to complicate her new life. And he'd thought she would be better off without him.

Abby respected his decision and never held any ill will toward him. But even after they'd reconnected, Walter had never offered to see her. She'd never asked why either. She'd always thought there would be plenty of time for visits in the future. Now she wondered if there was more to the story.

Once Walter was back in her life, they remained in regular contact with each other. It was also when he began sending Abby an envelope every year on her birthday. Delivered by courier, the envelope never showed a return address. Inside, there were always instructions for a treasure hunt.

One year, Walter had sent her a brochure of the Delaware Water Gap and a map of Monroe County, Pennsylvania. The hunt had forced her to head home for the first time since her residency had started at the hospital a year earlier. Various clues had led her to her parents' house. It had been Walter's way of telling Abby she needed a break from work and was long overdue to spend time with her family.

Why hadn't he confided in her that he'd had cancer? Things would have been different. She would have been there for him. But, Abby guessed that was the point. Walter wanted her to remember him as he was, not as a dying man in a veteran's hospital on the other side of the country. Abby's birthday was next month, and in her heart, she sensed this note—a three-word clue to find her sister—was Walter's way of giving her one final gift.

No one in her family comprehended how Abby could grieve for someone she hadn't seen since preschool when Walter had still had visitation rights—not that he'd used them very often. Even Wyatt didn't get it, and they were close. They shared a house. Her brother simply didn't understand what she was going through and tension had formed between them.

She sighed as she held her cell phone to her ear. "Hello, Mr. Tanner? My name's Abby Winchester. A woman named Kay referred you to me. I need your help finding my sister."

CLAY POCKETED HIS phone and turned to his best friend, Shane Langtry. "Your mom just sent a client my way."

"I hope this one pays you in something other than livestock," Shane joked as he helped Clay set a newly constructed roof on the chicken coop. "Any more animals and you'll need a second job to keep you in feed." He shook his head as he surveyed Clay's modest ranch.

"Isn't that the truth!"

"Keep your eye on that shelter over there." Shane pointed to the farthest pigpen. "The roof support looks like it's seen better days."

Clay nodded, thinking about the ideas he'd had for the ranch when he'd purchased it a few years earlier. Raised in a family that raised sheep for wool, he had intended to raise alpacas, hoping to bring his father aboard once he got the farm off the ground. Watching the man manage someone else's fiber mill when he knew his father's heart was elsewhere pained Clay. And he felt partly responsible for it.

Money had already been tight before Clay's birth,

and it had never seemed to get any better. When his sister, Hannah, had come along twelve years later, it had been even tighter. At a young age, Clay had picked up on his parents' financial struggles and had never asked for things that weren't necessary.

After Clay graduated high school, he knew his father was disappointed that Clay chose to study criminal justice instead of agriculture. His father had wanted him to help run the family business. Despite his disappointment, Gage Tanner had urged his son to follow his heart. It made sense. Wool production had been slowly declining in the United States. The industry wasn't nearly as profitable as it had been when Clay's great-grandparents had started sheep farming seventy-five years ago.

Halfway through his time away at college, Clay's parents had faced foreclosure. He'd offered to come home and help with the ranch, but his father told him it wouldn't change anything. Days before the bank had been ready to auction off the Tanners' land, they'd received a reprieve of sorts.

Their close relationship with the Langtrys had allowed his parents to keep the family home along with a handful of acres when Joe Langtry purchased the property. The sale had been enough to cover their debts, but the Tanners had been forced to sell off the sheep to other area farmers.

Clay knew the animals' fate bothered his mother. She had prided herself on the fiber processing mill she'd built from the ground up and it nearly killed her to watch her beloved sheep taken away by the truckload.

Clay had paid for college on his own with the aid of student loans, but that hadn't eased the regret he had for not being around when his father needed him most. Now

Clay wanted to regain some of that Tanner pride and raise alpacas, which were much more valuable for their fleece.

He shook his head. He'd never imagined wanting to follow in his father's and grandfather's footsteps, but life changed in a heartbeat—Clay was proof of that. The new ranch wouldn't be the same as the one his family had once owned, but it would be a chance to regain their rich history in fiber production.

Clay laughed to himself. He would have gotten somewhere with his dream if more of his private investigator clients actually paid him in cash.

It didn't matter that he told people his fees up front, the majority of the time they could barely afford his retainer. Farmers were having financial problems thanks to a multi-year drought and the ever-increasing amount of imported goods into the States. Unable to say no to the people he'd known his entire life, Clay had accepted animals as payment. He now owned a small herd of goats, more pigs than he cared to admit and enough chickens to warrant constructing an addition on the coop. He kept what he could afford, the rest he sold. Except for the chickens, which earned their keep by providing breakfast on most days. The remaining eggs his neighbor graciously sold for him at her farm stand. It didn't make him a great businessman, but helping his clients helped ease his conscience a bit. He had more than his share of sins to atone for.

"Thanks for helping me out this morning." Clay tugged off his gloves and shoved them in his back pocket, irritated that he'd allowed the past to disturb his thoughts. He kept himself constantly busy for that exact reason. To forget. "I need to clean up and head out to The Magpie to meet my potential client."

He enjoyed being a private investigator, which was

more than he'd anticipated. He had viewed it as a temporary layover after leaving his job at the Alcohol, Tobacco, Firearms and Explosives field office in Houston. Reuniting people was his favorite part of the job, something Clay knew he'd never have the chance to experience himself.

"Man or woman?" Shane asked.

"Woman." Clay snorted. "What does it matter?"

"A woman, huh?" Shane smiled and pushed his hat back. "Maybe she's hot, thinks her husband's cheating on her and is seeking revenge by having an affair with her private investigator."

"I think your wife has you watching too many Lifetime movies." Clay had never thought he'd see the day his friend would become a one-woman man, but marriage suited Shane.

"And I think you need a woman in your life."

"Just because you and Lexi got hitched last year doesn't mean the rest of us need or even want to walk down the aisle. Let it go. I'm fine."

"You're not fine." Shane removed his hat and wiped his brow with the back of his forearm. "Ever since you moved back to town, you've been a shell of who you used to be. I get it. Someone broke your heart, but come on, Clay, it's been almost three years and you haven't gone out with anyone. Hell, you haven't even unpacked your house yet. That's not normal."

Clay swallowed. "I've been busy." He averted his eyes from Shane's. It was more than a broken heart, though. He was still too raw to discuss with Shane, or anyone, what had happened to the only woman he'd ever loved. Clay hated the concern he saw in his friend's face. It wasn't necessary. He was fine—as long as he stayed busy, he was fine. Turning around, he grabbed his tools and tossed them into the five-gallon utility bucket. "Why are you bringing this up now? It hasn't bothered you before."

"Because I didn't realize how bad it still was until I went inside to use your bathroom earlier. It's the first time I've been inside your house in ages. You're always at our place. Your house hasn't changed since you moved in. What's going on?"

"Leave it alone, Shane." Clay spun and faced his friend. "I haven't decided what I'm doing with the house yet, and if I rip out the walls downstairs, I'd have to pack everything up anyway. Remodeling takes time and I don't have it right now."

Shane replaced his hat on top of his head and held up his hands. Despite his friend's gesture, Clay knew Shane wasn't buying his excuse.

"Say no more. Sorry I mentioned it. Just know if you need any help—remodeling—I'm here for you." He pointed to the chicken coop. "Let's nail the roof on before I go."

"I'll do it when I get back." Clay wanted this conversation to end—scratch that, he needed Shane to drop the subject…permanently. The sudden awkwardness between them seemed a mile wide. "I have to clean up and head out in a few. Thanks again for your help and I'll catch up with you later."

Clay headed for his 1940s farm house, leaving Shane no opportunity to say another word. He climbed up the porch stairs. Once inside, he closed the door and stared through the kitchen into the dark dining room. The room was filled with boxes instead of a dining table and chairs. He didn't own much, but whatever he did was in those boxes. So were the memories of the woman and child he loved more than anything. Their deaths were on his hands and Clay wasn't ready to let go…not yet.

I︫T︫ ︫W︫A︫S︫ ︫A︫F︫T︫E︫R︫ ︫L︫U︫N︫C︫H︫ when Abby poked her head through the entrance of The Magpie. The intoxicating aroma of fresh brewed coffee, baked bread and bacon enveloped her.

This is where he wants to meet me? A luncheonette?

"Don't be shy." A fiftysomething woman with a trendy layered bob called out as she entered the kitchen carrying an armful of dirty dishes. "Have a seat anywhere."

Not that there was anything wrong with meeting in a luncheonette, it just wasn't where Abby thought a P.I. should meet a client for the first time. For one, it wasn't private, and in her opinion, it wasn't professional, either. But Kay had raved about him. Though a stranger's word didn't really mean much, it was all she had to go on. Her heels clicked as she crossed the black-and-white checkerboard floor, the sound alerting her to how overdressed she was for somewhere this casual. She smoothed the front of her skirt and looked around.

The place was small and cozy with only a handful of people occupying the tables. Abby locked in on the man sitting at the counter. She was no private investigator, but she was willing to bet he was Clay Tanner.

The tightening in her chest at the sight of his angular jaw and tousled, sandy blond hair took her a bit off guard. His white long-sleeve Western shirt stretched across broad shoulders. A straw Stetson perched on the stool beside him.

Maybe there was something to Kay's matchmaking, after all.

Abby halted as a statuesque waitress leaned on the counter, her face close to Clay's. "And to what do I owe the pleasure of serving you twice today?" The ringlets of her ginger ponytail bounced with each word. Her pink uniform and white apron were a throwback to the fifties.

The outfit worked for her. Not many people could pull off that look.

"I'm meeting a client here," the man drawled.

Not one to miss a cue, Abby drew her five-foot-one-inch frame straighter—she was five-five if she included the heels—and approached the man.

"I believe you're waiting for me," Abby said.

He met her eyes and held them, not giving her the typical male once-over she usually received. Abby wasn't sure if she should be flattered or disappointed.

He's just polite. Real men don't treat women as objects.

Screw polite. Abby wanted to give *him* the once-over, but she maintained eye contact for fear that, if she didn't, she'd lose all control of her senses. She didn't want to start panting over the man!

"I'm Abby Winchester."

Deep sapphire-blue eyes flashed and somewhere in his face there was a hint of a smile. It made her wonder if he was one of those men who didn't want you to think they were interested in you, even though they really were.

He gestured to the waitress that he was moving to one of the vacant booths across from the counter, and then returned his attention to her. "Abby Winchester." The soothing way he said her name had her wanting to hear it again. He rose, long and lean, and held out his hand. Even with her wearing heels, he was a good foot taller than Abby. "Clay Tanner. It's a pleasure to meet you."

The warmth of his grip radiated up her arm, causing a slight tremor along her spine. He motioned for her to have a seat in the booth. She slid in, tugging at the hem of her short houndstooth skirt to prevent it from riding farther up her thighs and becoming a belt. Some clothes weren't meant for booth-scooting.

"Mr. Tanner." Abby removed a black-and-white file folder from her Balenciaga tote and pushed it across the table. "I'm afraid I don't have much to go on."

"Hi, I'm Bridgett. Welcome to The Magpie." Startled, Abby looked up at the woman. What she wouldn't give to have legs that long. The waitress placed two glasses of water on the table and handed her a menu.

Abby didn't need to look at it. She knew exactly what she wanted. The scent of bacon beckoned, causing her to crave her favorite sandwich.

"I'll have a BLT on white toast, mayo on the side and an order of fries." She returned the menu. "And a black coffee, please."

"Sure thing, hon," Bridgett said. "What about you, Clay? Bert made that jalapeño crawfish chowder you love so much."

"How can I say no?" He beamed at the waitress.

"Coming right up."

Abby followed Clay's eyes and was pleasantly surprised when they didn't wander to Bridgett's retreating backside. Was it possible gentlemen still existed?

"Designer folder?" Clay opened the black-and-white fleur-de-lis file, revealing its hot-pink lining. "Now I've seen it all."

"There is nothing wrong with being fashionably organized, Mr. Tanner." She had purposely purchased the folder at the stationer's to match the outfit she had chosen for their meeting. But now she felt silly.

"I'm not saying there is." He leaned back against the booth. "However, if we're going to work together, I insist you call me Clay. Mr. Tanner is my father."

"Agreed," Abby nodded. "Those are copies of my birth certificate and my father's death certificate."

Clay flipped through the pages. "Both documents list a different father."

"My mom remarried when I was two. My stepfather adopted me years later. Legally, it changed all my records naming him as my father, but it didn't sever my rights as Walter's next of kin. A copy of all court records and my adoption are in there."

"What makes you think you have a sister?"

"I arrived at the hospital the day after Walter died and a nurse gave me a handwritten note. She said he was adamant I received it. It said *find your sister*. Nothing more."

"Do you have the note?" Clay asked.

"On me? No." The piece of scrap paper was all Abby had left of her biological father. It was home, tucked safely in a drawer so she wouldn't lose it. She'd never thought to keep any of his treasure hunts. Then again, she'd never expected their time to end so soon. "I assure you, that's all there was."

"The note didn't seem strange to you at all?"

Abby blinked back tears. "No. Notes were our thing. Every year for my birthday, Walter sent me a clue and I had to search for my real gift. It was never anything of monetary value—it was always something much greater. I guess you could say this is my final clue, a few weeks before my birthday. I need to know what it means. I'm hoping you can help me figure it out."

"I promise to do my best." Clay rested his hand on top of hers. "I'm sorry for your loss."

His touch rocketed through her. The forwardness alone should have sent Abby in the other direction. Instead, she found his simple gesture comforting, understanding.

"Thank you. Ours was an unconventional relationship, and as strange as all this must sound, it worked for us. I had no idea he was sick until it was too late."

Clay gave her hand a brief squeeze before he withdrew and continued studying the contents of the folder. Instantly, Abby missed his touch and wanted to say, *please don't let go yet. Just a few more minutes.* But she needed to find the meaning of Walter's note, not send the man running in the opposite direction.

"I see you were born here," Clay said over the top of the folder.

"Walter was stationed at Randolph Air Force Base when I was born. My parents rented an apartment here in Ramblewood until on-base housing became available, but I'm not sure how long they lived here. My mom hasn't been very forthcoming with any information. I figured Ramblewood was the best place to start. I'm hoping you can find someone here who remembers them."

"How old is your sister?"

"Here you are." Bridgett set their food on the table. "Holler if you need anything else."

Abby inhaled the scent of her BLT. She twisted the top off the ketchup bottle and smacked the bottom of it until it poured onto her fries.

"I don't know how old she is, or if she exists."

Clay remained silent. Abby looked up to find him staring at her incredulously. She placed the bottle on the table and shrugged. "What? I like ketchup."

Eyes wide, he asked, "You don't know how old your sister is or if she's real?"

"This is all news to me. The nurse said my father wrote the note hours before he died. Deathbed confessions being what they are, I thought there might be something to it. Although my mother and father—I call my stepdad my father because he raised me so he earned that title—never heard of any sister. My mom says if one existed, she would have known about her since she had

remained in contact with his family. Given that Walter
was in the service and stationed overseas for a while,
anything is possible."

"So I'm looking for a woman in no particular age
range, possibly not even in this country, who may or
may not exist?"

"I know this is a long shot. Logic tells me she's
younger—maybe there was someone else after my mom
and Walter split, although no one I've spoken with on his
side of the family knows anything, either. A part of me
wonders if this is why my parents divorced. Mom has
been quick to dismiss it, which makes me even more
curious."

Clay didn't respond. He ate a few spoonfuls of chowder and reviewed the documents along with the sparse
notes she had jotted down. Abby dove into her sandwich,
studying him.

If she'd met Clay on the street, she wouldn't have
guessed he was a private investigator. Physically, he
was more the actor or country singer type with his high
cheekbones and the dark blond stubble along his jawline.
Clean-cut meets cowboy. He was definitely easy on the
eyes, and Abby wondered why he was still single. Not
that it was any of her business, but Kay had made it a
point to tell her that much.

"Before I take a case," he said. "I have to let you know
in advance that I run a background check on all my clients. It's standard practice, so if there's anything you
need to tell me, please let me know now."

"I have nothing to hide."

Clay regarded her from across the table, and she fidg-
eted in her seat. She knew she probably appeared desperate, but she needed Clay to help find out if her father's
message was true. With only two weeks off from work,

Abby was on a definite time crunch. Even if Walter hadn't written the note, she needed the break from the hospital. And, it gave her time to plan her next animal-assisted therapy proposal. Giving up wasn't an option when her patients' well-being was at stake.

Clay cleared his throat and she met his questioning look. "Assuming nothing turns up in your background check, I'll start with the court house and military records to see what I can discover. Do you know how long he was stationed at Randolph Air Force Base?"

Abby shook her head. She didn't have much information to offer him. Her internet searches on her biological dad hadn't turned up anything.

"Do you always meet your clients here?" she asked, taking another bite of her sandwich.

"I meet them wherever it's convenient. I don't have an office, per se. I have clients scattered throughout this and the neighboring counties so I usually go to them."

"I couldn't find any record of you online," she said, in between bites of her fries.

Clay laughed and pulled a napkin from the chrome dispenser on the table. He wiped his mouth. "Investigating me now, huh?"

"I'm hiring you to handle a significant matter. If this sister exists, it will change both of our lives, so yes, I did some research on you."

"Well, it's definitely a challenging case, but if she's out there, I'll do everything in my power to find her. Just be forewarned of one thing. If I do locate her and she doesn't want you to have her contact information, I can't give it to you."

Abby almost dropped her sandwich. "That hardly seems fair. What kind of backwards law is that?"

"Technically it's not, but it should be. It's strictly

ethics based—my ethics—and any investigator worth his or her salt will tell you the same thing. You have no idea how many cases I've turned away because an abusive husband is trying to find out where his wife ran off to with the kids. That's why most investigators run a background check on their clients first."

"I guess that makes sense." Abby hated to think Clay could possibly unearth the answers she wanted and then not share them with her. "Kay speaks highly of you, and although I just met her today, I'm taking her word for it. But it still doesn't explain why I couldn't find you online."

Clay grinned, his left brow rising a fraction. "Kay's been a second mother to me and one of the nicest people you'll ever meet. I swear I spent more time at her house than I did at my own when I was growing up. Now that I think about, it still holds true today. To help ease your mind, I'm a retired Alcohol, Tobacco and Firearms field agent turned private investigator. The reason I'm not online is because I don't advertise. I rely solely on word of mouth. Did Kay happen to mention anything else while she was at it?"

Abby swore she saw a slight tinge of color spread across Clay's face, and she wasn't sure if it was the jalapeño chowder or the question itself. Either way, she found it endearing.

"Kay made a point to tell me you're single."

"I had a feeling she did." The edges of his mouth curled upward as he kept his eyes on his lunch. "I love her to death, but she's a bit of a matchmaker."

"How's my favorite customer this morning?" The woman who had greeted Abby when she first arrived stood at the edge of the booth, patting Clay's shoulder. Her laugh lines deepened as she grinned. "If you talk to your momma today, tell her to stop in. I made her favorite rum-vanilla cream pie."

"Will do." Clay turned to Abby. "Abby Winchester, this is Maggie Dalton, The Magpie's infamous owner."

"Infamous!" the woman howled. "I'm a lot of things, but none of them infamous. It's a pleasure to meet you, Abby. I hope you enjoy your stay in Ramblewood."

"It's nice to meet you, too." Abby shook the woman's hand. "Did you say rum-vanilla cream pie? Sounds scrumptious."

"Oh, honey, let me cut you a slice." Maggie rushed off to the kitchen before Abby could object, which was fine by her. She was never one to turn down a slice of pie.

"She seems nice." Abby reached into her bag and handed Clay a prewritten check, confident Kay had sent her in the right direction. "This is your retainer. And, yes, I'm paying you now because you won't find anything derogatory about me when you do your background search. I added a little more than what we discussed over the phone because I don't want the possibility of extra expenses causing any delays."

Clay took a sip of coffee and folded her check in half, tucking it into his shirt pocket. "I won't know what we're looking at until I start digging around. When we spoke on the phone, you mentioned you'd only be in town for two weeks. I can't promise I'll have anything by then. There are quite a few unknown factors in this case, but I'll give you a status update every couple of days."

"Here you go." Maggie placed two slices of pie in front of them. "It's on me, welcoming you to town."

Abby smiled. "Thank you." The scents of vanilla bean and rich custard wafted upward. If she could, she'd bottle the scent and bathe in it. She ran the side of her fork through the tip of the slice and lifted it to her mouth.

Whipped cream melted into rum, with a slight tang that danced across her tongue.

"Oh, Maggie." Abby's eyes closed in bliss. "This is amazing. Thank you."

"You're welcome, dear. Enjoy." The woman left them to their dessert.

"Uh-oh," Clay teased. "The Magpie has claimed another victim. You will forever crave Maggie's pies from this point forward."

"I swear." Abby waved her fork above the pie, taking another bite. "This is better than sex."

"I'll admit, it's pretty darn good, but darling, if you think pie is better than sex, you're doing it all wrong." He winked.

Abby folded her arms across her chest and laughed. "You may just have a point there."

She finished her pie, then dabbed at her mouth with a napkin. "I'm staying at Mazie's Bed and Biscuit if you need me. I wrote my cell number on the inside of the folder even though I'm sure you already have it on your phone. I'll leave you to your work."

She swung her legs out from under the table, holding on to her skirt for dear life. *Note to self, wear booth-appropriate clothing for future meetings.* When she pulled her wallet from her bag, Clay rose and placed his hand on hers. There was that damn surge through her body again.

"Lunch is on me." Clay's hand lingered, giving hers another gentle squeeze. "I'll be in touch soon."

Abby fought the urge to reach up and give him a thank-you kiss, but thought better of it. No need to embarrass herself. His touch felt warm and comfortable, and after the past month, she needed human contact. She needed a hug, dammit—but she'd settle for this—for now.

THE CURVE OF Abby's toned calves caught Clay's eye as she headed for the door. How in the world she teetered on heels that high was beyond him. However, he appreciated the way they made her legs seem endless. The short skirt she wore added to the effect. What she lacked in height, Abby Winchester made up in confidence.

Although she was a bit too fancy for these parts, she definitely made the blood pump through his veins a little faster. But Abby was a client, and he knew enough not to mix business with pleasure. He'd made that mistake once and he'd have to live with the aftermath of it for the rest of his life.

Kay had sent Abby his way and now he wondered if it was because she thought he was the man for the job or if she thought he was the man for Abby. He didn't understand why the Langtrys had a sudden interest in his love life. It wouldn't be fair for any woman to get involved with him, not when he had nothing left to give.

Regardless of Kay's reasons, Clay had a job to do, and until it was complete, he wasn't going to lose sight of who Abby was. A client. He just wished she hadn't run off so quickly after they had finished their pie. Another cup of coffee would have given him the opportunity to ask her a little more about her family and herself…purely for investigative purposes.

Clay had to admit, this was definitely his most difficult locate case since he'd become a private investigator. Nothing like zero information to go on. He redirected his attention to the papers before him. In a small town like Ramblewood, someone was bound to remember Abby's family.

"Refill?" Bridgett held the pot over his cup.

"Yes, please." Bridgett Jameson—here was a woman any man would be lucky to settle down with. His friend

Jon Reese had a crush on her. If she'd only give the poor guy a chance. "Are you sure you won't let Jon take you to the movies this weekend?"

"I'm sorry, Clay, he's not the one," she called over her shoulder, walking behind the counter.

The one. Clay had had his *one* and he'd lost her. He admired Bridgett for holding out, and he hoped once she found him, she held on tight. Life was too short, too fragile. In a matter of seconds, it could blow up in your face, taking all you loved with it.

Chapter Two

"He's definitely single," Mazie said over breakfast the next morning as she and Abby sat at the large dining table with a few of the other guests. "I don't think he's dated anyone since he moved back to town a few years ago."

"Interesting." Abby fiddled with her fork.

"I'm willing to bet if you head down the road to Slater's Mill tonight, you'll find him there, but you didn't hear that from me."

"Slater's Mill?" An unexplained wave of anticipation washed over Abby at the thought of seeing Clay again.

"It's a little honky-tonk a few blocks away. They have a big dance floor and there's a band playing most nights. Just continue down Shelby and you'll see it on your left. If you cross Cooter Creek you went too far."

Abby immediately tried to visualize her clothing options, realizing her suitcase didn't offer much by way of evening clothes. A social life after the sun set had never crossed her mind, so she had packed knitting needles and yarn, instead. She wasn't usually this unprepared. She habitually overpacked when traveling. But once she'd decided to head to Ramblewood, she had focused solely on finding her sister, not the local bar scene.

"Is there any place I can buy something to wear tonight?"

"There's Cowpokes across the street, but that's more Western wear. You look more like the Margarita's Rag-patch type. It's one block down past the cleaner's and Promise Travel. Big store, you can't miss it."

"Thanks for your help."

Why did she care what she wore in front of a man she wouldn't be around long enough to know much about? Between problems at work and the search for her sister, she didn't have room in her life for a relationship, even a temporary one. If she were being honest with herself, though, she'd never felt more alone than she did now. Abby sensed Clay understood where she was coming from.

There had been a look of recognition in his eyes when she'd told him about Walter. His comforting touch had given Abby the impression he'd gone through similar grief.

Anyway, what was wrong with some much-needed, lighthearted fun—with the opposite sex? Normally, the thought of hitting a club was a drag, but that was because her coworkers and Wyatt usually brought dates.

After Abby found a dress and boots at Margarita's Ragpatch, she headed back to the Bed & Biscuit. Perched on the edge of her four-poster bed, Duffy rested along-side her, exhausted from another afternoon romp at the Bark Park.

The room was larger than she had envisioned it would be when she had read the online brochure. Quintessential Victorian, yet one hundred percent pet safe. A romantic, floral stencil covered the walls, which meant no loose wallpaper seams to entice curious animals to pull.

On the bed laid a heavily embossed, yet easily laundered *matelassé* coverlet. Every piece of furniture was tall, with open access underneath for pets to retreat to, if they so pleased. Bed steps allowed older pets, and more petite guests, to settle in for the evening with little effort—a feature Abby was particularly happy to see. Needing a running head start in order to leap into bed was not her idea of a nightcap.

Safety covers protected electrical outlets so wayward paws and curious noses didn't poke where they shouldn't. The room was free of lace so small nails wouldn't snag. Nothing dangled to beguile its furry occupants.

Pet guests received a Mazie's Bed & Biscuit placemat under their elevated food dishes. Amenities included fresh food bowls twice daily, filtered spring water and a dog-walking service, in case a pet owner was out longer than expected. Mazie brought the term *creature comforts* to an entirely new level, emphasizing the importance of pets to their human counterparts. Abby could use more people like Mazie on the hospital board, then maybe she'd get somewhere.

"I wish I had some answers, Duffy." Soft snores emanated from the stretched-out form next to her. "Oh, sure, sleep your way through my troubles."

Abby hated the abrupt way she had left her job the other day, but the combination of her defeat and Walter's note had gotten the best of her. A break to reevaluate her situation was in order.

Physical therapy was her lifeblood, and she wanted to give her patients every opportunity to improve *their* lives. She had devoted seven years of school and two years in the field to helping others, and she refused to settle. She just hadn't found the winning combination to sway the hospital to use pet therapy, but Abby was confident they'd see things her way eventually. Failure was not an option.

She checked the clock. It was an hour later in South Carolina than Ramblewood, but she took the chance her supervisor would still be working. The phone rang twice. "Physical Therapy, Angela speaking."

"Hello, it's Abby." She peeked out the window and admired a couple holding hands as they crossed the street. "How are my patients doing?"

"Hey, girl." Angela's voice sounded tired. "They're good. They keep asking about you, though. You did take off rather suddenly."

"I know, but it couldn't be helped. Please tell everyone I'm thinking of them. Has there been any further improvement with Donald Davis?"

"Some," Angela sighed. "Although he isn't as cooperative with the other therapists."

Abby groaned. She felt horrible for abandoning her patients without explanation, but she knew they were in capable hands. Her colleagues were some of the best in the state, and many of them supported her bid for animal-assisted therapy. No matter their qualifications, some of her long-term inpatients had a harder time adjusting to another therapist. And in Donald's case, he had a tendency to get downright ornery with anyone other than Abby.

"Donald has more respect for people who don't let him get away with any crap, despite the arguments that may ensue. You just let him know I expect him to be on his best behavior or he'll have to answer to me when I return." That alone should bring a smile to the elderly man's face. "I know I left everyone in the lurch, but I had to do this."

"I know you did." Angela was more than her supervisor, she was a close friend. "How are you doing?"

"You know me." Abby paced to the other side of the room. "Keeping busy. I'm in Texas following up on Walter's mystery note."

"Oh Abby," Angela said. "Are you sure that's a good idea?"

"I came here to find answers. I may or may not be looking in the right place, but at least I'm doing something about it instead of playing the wondering game."

Abby sat on the bed steps, drawing her knees to her chest. She'd been a toddler when her mother had married Steve Winchester, and she had no recollection of the event. The day her brother was born five years later, though, that was another story. She'd never forget that wonderful day. Abby had doted on Wyatt from the beginning. Although, she had always felt like an outsider when she saw him and their parents together. Wyatt was *their* biological child, and even though Steve had raised her as his own, it still bothered Abby that she'd never know the feeling of belonging the way Wyatt did. There were too many what-ifs surrounding Walter's note and she was afraid they'd consume her if she didn't look for the truth.

"I hope you find what you're looking for." Angela's words competed with another voice through the phone. Hearing a muffled sound, Abby suspected that Angela had covered the mouthpiece. "I'm sorry, I have to go. You'd better keep me posted."

"I will." Abby hung up, climbed onto the bed and lay back on the pillows. She missed her patients, the interaction, the progress they made and the determination that drove them further each day. But she wasn't about to feel sorry for herself. She'd witnessed far too many of her patients battling horrific injuries and overcoming major obstacles so they could live fully again. Their situations were why Abby refused to allow the phrase *self-pity* to enter her vocabulary.

She glanced at her snoozing dog. "I think you have the right idea, Duffy."

Abby closed her eyes, and her thoughts immediately drifted to Clay. Naturally, she had noticed how tall, muscular and downright sexy he was, but more importantly, he held the key to her future. Abby thought back to what Clay had told her at The Magpie. If he found her sister, the woman may not want Abby to know anything about her. Abby's search would be over without a single answer. That scenario had never crossed her mind. Could she live with that? Abby didn't think so.

She turned onto her side and ran her hand down Duffy's back. Maybe Kay did have a point about exploring what Ramblewood had to offer. Abby wouldn't mind running into the *single* P.I. tonight. Maybe he'd show her around the town her parents had once called home. Ramblewood was part of her past and she might as well make the best of her trip.

The shrill of her cell phone startled her. The number for CT Investigations splayed across the screen. Had Clay found her sister already?

AFTER SEARCHING THE courthouse and town hall for information about Abby's sister—and turning up nothing—Clay headed home. Fortunately, he had managed to wrap up another case, so at least the trip wasn't a total loss. Placing Abby's ornate file folder on the counter, he groaned. Why couldn't he shake her from his mind? He dug his phone out of his pocket and flipped open the folder. Before he could change his mind about calling, Abby answered.

"So soon?" Her voice burst through the earpiece.

"Excuse me?" Clay asked. What did she mean by *soon?* Did he break one of those female rules that said he had to wait a certain amount of time before calling?

They'd had a lunch meeting, not a date. He didn't think those rules applied here.

"I can't believe you have something already," Abby said. "Did you find my sister?"

"Um, no. Nothing yet." Clay's jaw clenched, already chastising himself for what he was about to ask. "I wondered if you'd be interested in grabbing a bite to eat. I wanted to discuss your family a little more to see if there's something you hadn't thought of before."

"Sure, that sounds fun." Clay detected Abby's enthusiasm over the phone. Was it because he had called, or was she simply bored with Ramblewood's limited tourist activities? Not that it mattered. Once again, he reminded himself she was a client. Her enthusiasm or lack thereof was of no concern to him. "Where did you have in mind?" she asked.

"Depends what you're in the mood for. We may not have much to do around here, but our Cooter Creek Restaurant Row draws crowds from clear across the county. There's Cajun, French, Mexican, German, sushi and steak. Then around Main Street we have Chinese, pizza and your standard burgers and fries fare."

"I'm absolutely jonesing for some Chinese, if that's okay with you. It's my favorite."

Amused by her expression, Clay didn't think the phrase "jonesing" came from South Carolina. Must be a part of her northeastern upbringing. "Chinese it is. Six o'clock all right? I'll pick you up at the Bed and Biscuit."

"Sounds wonderful."

"I'll see you then." Clay hung up the phone and banged his head repeatedly against the kitchen cabinet. "Why did I do that? I had no business calling her. This is a job, she's a client and I'm an idiot."

Yet he hadn't been able to get Abby out of his head

since meeting her yesterday. The woman had gotten under his skin and he hadn't allowed that to happen since Ana Rosa. His fiancée's face had begun to fade from his dreams lately, and though he tried to hang on to every memory of her, some days they began to blur. The thought of losing her memory terrified him. If only he'd done things differently and told her the truth. There were no second chances, though. Both Ana Rosa and her son were dead. And it was his fault.

Clay grabbed a beer from the fridge and glanced around his old farmhouse. Shane was right, it hadn't changed much since the day he bought the place. Well, maybe he had opened a box or two when he'd been searching for a particular item. It had been so long since he'd looked inside any of the boxes, he had trouble remembering what he owned.

Clay had entertained thoughts of donating everything to the local thrift shop. And why not? After surviving this many years without the boxes' contents, he obviously didn't need whatever was inside. But he knew one of those boxes contained their photos. Reminders of the days they'd spent together, promises he'd made to them of a future and a life free of fear. All of them broken— every single promise—irretrievably broken.

"Dammit!" Clay kicked at the screen door and stormed down the back porch stairs. Heading for the barn, he passed all his clients' payments, including his newly acquired five-year-old Welsh pony, Olivia. Originally, he had planned to give the mare away, but when his gelding Dream Catcher had met Olivia, it was love at first sight.

At a little under thirteen hands, she was much smaller than his Morgan horse, but their silver-dappled coloring was almost identical. Clay figured the two were meant to be together. Once again, Abby came to mind—she was much shorter than he was.

"Get a grip, Clay." He led both horses from the corral into the barn. "Abby's not a pony and I'm sure as hell no gelding."

Frustrated that he had let the slightest bit of Abby seep into his thoughts, he placed Dream Catcher in his stall. When he returned from feeding the goats, the horse stood in the middle of the barn, ears twitching and tail swishing as if he were about to bolt.

He'd forgotten to latch the door. Allowing Abby to cloud his vision had already complicated his life. His horse could be in danger if Clay couldn't corral him back into the stall. The last thing he needed was to chase Dream Catcher down the two-lane road that was only a stone's throw from the barn.

"Are you seriously going to do this to me today?" Clay held his arms wide attempting to make himself appear larger. He was afraid to close the barn doors behind him for fear the horse would turn and run out the other side of the building. If Dream Catcher ran straight for him, Clay at least had a better chance of catching the animal. "Come on, pal. You don't want to leave your girlfriend here all alone, do you?"

Slowly, Clay inched forward. Dream Catcher lowered his head slightly and for a second, Clay wondered if the gelding was about to charge. Reaching for the lariat hanging on the barn wall, Clay hoped he had enough clearance to throw it before the horse turned and bolted.

Dream Catcher snorted and stomped his hoof, then nonchalantly walked into his stall.

"Are you kidding me?" Clay quickly latched the door. "What was that—a test? I've had enough of those today, thank you."

Tests he was apparently failing. Why had he opened his big mouth and asked the pint-size blonde out to dinner?

Because he lacked enough good sense to keep his distance.

He lived a quiet, uncomplicated life, and that's how he wanted to keep it. The last thing he needed was Abby Winchester and her problems...only the fact that no one else knew of a sister didn't sit right with him. Locate cases rarely resulted in a neatly wrapped gift box full of answers. Instead, they had a tendency to take on a life of their own with the subject of the search usually secreted for a reason. Clay's gut told him Abby's life was about to unravel. And that bothered him much more than it should have.

Abby had passed New China earlier in the day and knew the dress she had bought at Margarita's Ragpatch would be overkill for the tiny, ultracasual restaurant. It was definitely a low-key type of place. She slipped into her favorite curve-hugging distressed jeans and topped them off with a cotton and lace empire-waist sleeveless shirt under a soft peach linen cropped jacket. As she rolled up her sleeves and slid some wooden bangles onto her wrists, she decided on a pair of platform chocolate-leather ankle booties.

Her mother's words whenever they went shopping echoed through Abby's head. *Neutral pieces will carry you everywhere. You can always accessorize.* Her mother, queen of the cruise lines, knew how to dress to impress. Her parents were perpetually off to some exciting locale. They were on second honeymoon number one thousand at this point. Wyatt and Abby never joined them, not even when they had been kids. Their grandparents had taken care of them while Maeve and Steve sailed off into the sunset.

Abby admired their relationship. They were one of those perfectly in sync couples who finished each other's sentences, and she was willing to bet they were as much in love today as they were when they met. Maybe more. Abby dreamed of the day she'd find her soul mate. She'd been planning her wedding ever since she was a little girl. But a wedding would never happen unless she cleared her schedule a bit and actually took the time to meet someone.

Downstairs, she told Mazie she was going out for the evening. Mazie said she'd look in on Duffy and take him for a walk if Abby was gone for more than a few hours. Mazie's devotion to her pet guests more than justified the higher cost of staying at the Bed & Biscuit, in Abby's opinion. Many hotels didn't take pets and fewer offered dog-walking services.

Abby decided to wait for Clay on the Victorian's expansive wraparound porch. White antique rocking chairs invited guests to relax among the fall flowers in various sized pots and hanging baskets decorating the porch's perimeter. Serenity and intoxicating florals welcomed you to the Hill Country region of Texas the second you stepped out the door.

"You look very pretty, dear."

Abby jumped at the sound of a woman's voice. "You scared me." Abby hadn't noticed Janie Anderson, one of the inn's employees, standing in the corner of the porch with a watering can in her hand. "And thank you."

"I'm sorry." The older woman continued to water the plants while she spoke. "You can get lost in Mazie's jungle of flowers out here. I hear you have a date with our Mr. Tanner this evening."

Well that didn't take long to spread around. "I wouldn't

call it a date. We're meeting over dinner to discuss my mysterious sister."

"Yes, I've heard. Sounds exciting. I'm sorry I don't remember your parents from back then. I even looked through some of my old photos last night. My husband, Alfred, is an avid hobby photographer and I swear we have stacks of photos from every parade and festival Ramblewood's ever seen. Of course, I don't know what I'm looking for, either, but you are more than welcome to look through whatever we have."

"Really?" Maybe she'd find a photo of her parents, or one of her father and another child. "That's very generous of you."

"Any time you want to come over, you let me know. I can't say my Alfred is the most organized man, but the photos are in some semblance of order."

Abby couldn't wait to tell Clay the exciting news. Maybe the newspaper archives would have something about her father, too, but she was certain Clay would look into that on his own. Still, it wouldn't hurt to mention it.

A week ago, Ramblewood, Texas, hadn't been a blip on her radar. She'd arrived in town so quickly she had a hard time distinguishing one day from the next. Now that she was here, thoughts she hadn't considered complicated the situation.

Did her sister have a relationship with Walter? Did they see each other often? Maybe Abby wasn't the only one he sent notes to. And maybe his yearly scavenger hunts weren't just for her.

"Are you all right?" Janie motioned for Abby to sit in one of the rockers.

"I'm sorry." She needed to escape her own head for a bit. She sat and Janie joined her. "I guess the reality of the situation is finally hitting me. To be honest, I thought it already had. I mean, the first big step was coming here, right? Then when I hired Clay, I thought *that* was the big step. In actuality, they're all little steps to finding the truth. The idea of having a sister that I never knew of is very surreal."

"If it's any consolation, I think you're handling yourself beautifully," Janie said.

"Thank you. When I first considered hiring an investigator I had my doubts anything would come of this. It was more wishful thinking, but when I was sitting in the Bark Park and then walking around town, I got this feeling—an indescribable draw that was telling me this is where I'm supposed to be." Abby looked up to see Janie listening intently. "I must sound crazy, but in my heart, I know it's only a matter of time before Clay finds the answers and then what? How do you make up for all that lost time?"

"You take it day by day, dear." Janie rested her hand on Abby's knee. "Don't worry about what happens next. Concentrate on what you do know so you can find her."

"I don't mean to sound pitiful. I haven't allowed myself to think about the end result, and it's kind of hitting me all at once."

"That's normal," Janie said. "I would say it's part of the grieving process over your father, too. Allow yourself to feel, but don't cross the line into dwelling on it."

Abby knew Janie was right. Seeing patients with disabilities and traumatic injuries every day, she had learned to appreciate everything she had. One of her old professors used to say, "As long as you're aboveground, there's always a bright side." Abby lived by those words. They were why she never allowed her patients to give up, even when they suffered a setback.

But one question had plagued Abby since she had

received Walter's note. Why would anyone keep her sister's existence a secret?

CLAY PULLED HIS TRUCK into the Bed & Biscuit parking lot. He shut off the engine and sat with the keys in his hand. He swallowed drily. This was dinner to discuss Abby's case, nothing more.

Then why did he need to keep reminding himself it wasn't a date? Because he *wanted* it to be a date and that made him feel worse than his nerves did.

Clay was attracted to Abby more than he cared to admit. When her background check revealed she was a physical therapist, he'd been intrigued. He had figured her more the clothing-designer type. Or an art dealer, maybe. A physical therapist was completely unexpected.

He inhaled deeply in a vain attempt to steady his uneven pulse. Failing miserably, he climbed from his mud-caked truck, cursing himself for not washing it. He proceeded around to the front of the inn where Abby waited for him in one of the rocking chairs. The warmth of her smile was echoed in her eyes. She met him halfway down the stairs, and he once again wondered how she managed to remain upright in such high heels. She looked beautiful in an effortless way.

Clay hoped he had the sense to keep that opinion to himself. Abby was a client and he refused to cross that line.

You already have.

"Are you ready to go?" Clay's voice broke. Abby's eyes widened slightly, but fortunately she let it slide without comment. Clay hadn't been remotely close to this nervous since the night he had proposed to Ana Rosa. A perpetual reminder that he couldn't blur the lines between client and romance. Not that romance was on the table. He wouldn't tarnish Ana Rosa's memory by having a fling with Abby, or anyone else for that matter.

Abby faced the sidewalk. "Since it's so beautiful out tonight, do you mind if we walk? It's still beastly humid back home and I'm loving this Texas weather."

"You want to walk to New China in those shoes?" Clay didn't think she'd make it fifty feet, let alone all the way down Main Street.

"I assure you I'll be fine. I'm quite capable of putting one foot in front of the other."

"Don't those things hurt your feet?" Clay opened the wrought-iron gate leading to the sidewalk and held it for Abby.

"Listen, I usually wear sneakers when I'm at work, and anything without a heel makes me feel like a twelve-year-old. Scratch that, most preteens are taller than I am. I wear heels so I can at least look like a grownup."

"If you say so." Clay found himself scrambling to keep up with her quick pace. "Are we race walking?"

Abby stopped and stared at him. "I'm sorry. I have to remind myself I'm not in a hurry to be anywhere while I'm here. My schedule is usually packed and I tend to run nonstop. I assume you completed my background search. Did I check out okay?"

Yes, you managed to check right into my every waking thought. "I was surprised to discover you're a physical therapist."

"What were you expecting…a personal shopper?" Abby teased. "Most people don't peg me for a PT because of my size, but if there's one thing I've learned over the years working with my patients, the only limitations are within your heart. I may be small, but I can do anything I put my mind to."

Clay admired Abby's confidence. He wished some of

it would rub off on him tonight because while she appeared composed, he was the exact opposite.

He'd worked undercover in dangerous sting operations and helped take down some of the country's most dangerous criminals, all while managing to keep his nerves in check. Yet a simple walk with an attractive client left him jumpier than spit on a hot skillet. It didn't help that the more Abby spoke of her work, the more impressed he became. By the time they were ready to order their dinner, he found himself captivated by the stories she told about her patients.

"I'll have the chicken lo mein, no mushrooms, and an egg roll, please." Abby handed her menu to the waiter.

Clay enjoyed a woman who ate real food and didn't pick at a salad while he chowed down on General Tso's shrimp and fried rice.

"I take it you're using your vacation time to come to Ramblewood." A part of Clay wished she'd be called back to work on some emergency so his heart rate could return to normal.

"It wasn't exactly planned. I basically decided I needed to get away from the hospital for a few weeks." Abby dipped a crunchy noodle into a small bowl of duck sauce and popped it into her mouth. "We're not exactly seeing eye to eye right now."

"About what?" Clay knew he should steer his questions toward her family, but curiosity drove him to ask why she needed a break from a job she clearly enjoyed.

"Animal-assisted therapy. My dog, Duffy, is a therapy pet, and we make the rounds of nursing homes and rehab centers. Just having a dog present transforms a room into something more familiar than a hospital bed and beeping machines. A brain tumor patient had been in ICU for a month and wouldn't open her eyes or react to any stimuli until we brought Duffy in. We put a sheet on the bed and he climbed up and lay beside her. Instantly, this woman put her hand on Duffy and opened her eyes. It was a life-changing experience for me. I've been trying to persuade the hospital to induct a program of its own."

"How's that going?"

"They've rejected my proposal three times. They would need to dedicate a team to research the program first. They feel it would cost too much money. Money they'd rather spend on conventional therapy with years of scientific study behind it." Abby broke a noodle in half and tossed it onto the table. "I told them I had already conducted a preliminary inquiry on the grants available and I'm willing to chair any events that would bring in donations to the program."

"Can you manage to take all of that on yourself?" Based on the determined lift of her chin and the challenge of her gaze, Clay knew the answer before she responded.

"I know it won't be easy, but I'm willing to do whatever it takes. This is personal for me. When I was a kid, I stuttered horribly. Other kids made fun of me. Everyone was always telling me to *think* before I spoke, which only made things worse." She shrugged. "I didn't have a problem thinking. I had a problem getting the words out of my mouth. My speech therapist told me to talk to my dog, alone, with no one else around, and you know what? I didn't stutter when it was just Ebony and me." Abby laughed. "I'm not saying that talking to him cured me, but it taught me to have confidence in myself. And, I still have my moments and my bad days when I stumble over my words, but who doesn't? I've had dogs my entire life and they've gotten me through some rough times." Her face suddenly reddened. "Wow, I'm monopolizing the conversation."

"No, you're not." The waiter set their meals on the table. Clay had intended to discuss Abby's family, but his interest in the woman became more personal the more she spoke about her work. "You remember the woman that referred you to me, Kay Langtry? She runs the Dance of Hope Hippotherapy Center, where they use the horses' movements to treat people with injuries and disabilities. I think you'd find it fascinating. I'm sure she'd love to give you a behind-the-scenes tour."

Abby bumped her water glass, sloshing some of it onto the table in her excitement. "You're kidding me!" She used her napkin to clean up the mess, and continued talking without missing a beat. "I never thought to look up animal-assisted therapy centers while I was here. I would love to see the place. Kay had told me she owned a ranch and to ask anyone in town to show me the way."

"I'd be happy to take you." Clay felt his stomach knot the moment he said the words. He'd crossed the line. Again. The desire to see her expression when she saw Dance of Hope and the therapy they provided almost made him want to clear his schedule tomorrow and drive her out there first thing. If he were smart, he'd give her directions and send her on her way, but logic had escaped him the moment he'd asked her to dinner.

"I'd love that. Thank you."

Abby beamed—her face literally glowed with anticipation, and in that instant, Clay realized his attraction to her was more than the superficial desire he had originally thought. Despite her glitzy exterior, she was one of the more down-to-earth and genuine people he'd met in ages.

Clay watched Abby masterfully twirl her lo mein noodles with her chopsticks, a feat he never thought possible. The woman continued to surprise him every minute. The fact she had volunteered to be a part of a Doctors

Without Borders physical therapy program in Ghana, Africa, last year warmed a place in his heart he hadn't known still existed.

He needed to reel himself in. The woman was a client and he was not about to let her down. He forced himself to focus on her family history throughout the rest of the meal. Abby was able to answer questions about everyone except her biological father because she knew very little about the man. Despite their contact over the years, Walter hadn't been very forthcoming. It wasn't the end of the world for Clay. It just made his job more difficult.

He didn't mind having Abby around for a little longer, though. While a simple open-and-shut case appealed to some private investigators, Clay loved a challenge, and Abby's case was definitely that. But she was awakening a part of him he had resolved would never see the light of day. Abby was in town for two weeks, and that was it. There was no chance of anything more than a brief acquaintance. Once the case was closed, Abby would leave for Charleston and he'd probably never see her again. Why didn't that thought sit well with him?

"The best part of the meal is the fortune cookies." Abby eagerly cracked hers open. *"The skills you have gathered will one day come in handy.* Oh, well, that's good to know."

Clay laughed and split his cookie in half, removing his fortune. *"There are many new opportunities that are being presented to you."* That one hit a little too close to home. He didn't want to think about new opportunities. He'd trade everything he had for Ana Rosa and Paulo to come back to him. The immediate guilt washing him over their deaths reminded him that a relationship with Abby was out of the question. Clay didn't deserve a second chance at happiness when Ana Rosa and Paulo didn't have a second chance at life. He cleared his throat. "It's getting late. We should head back. I have to be in court tomorrow morning."

Abby checked her watch. Clay knew it was barely eight o'clock and his excuse was lame, but if things went further, he'd never forgive himself. He had a feeling it would be easy to lose himself with the pint-size blonde. He wasn't ready for this, and he certainly wasn't ready for Abby.

Chapter Three

"Hit me again." Abby tapped two fingers next to her coffee cup.

"Your eyes look like two cherries in the snow," Bridgett said. "Didn't you get any sleep?"

"The last time I stayed up so late was when I studied for my state board exams."

Bridgett grinned. "Did someone keep you company last night?" She refilled Abby's empty cup.

"He sure did." Abby looked around to ensure no one else was listening. "He snuggled right beside me while I worked."

"Worked?" The waitress set the coffee carafe on the counter. If the woman were a puppy her ears would have stood up.

"Yes," Abby said, amused. "I'm a physical therapist, and I was researching animal-assisted therapy centers with my dog curled up next to me all night." Unfortunately, there weren't any facilities nearby, and outside of what she had read online about Dance of Hope, nothing compared to the program she would like to create in Charleston.

"Oh, and here I thought it was something exciting." Bridgett frowned. "Not that what you do isn't exciting. I'm sure it is. Before I stick my foot farther down my throat, can I get you something to eat?"

"No, thank you. At the rate I'm going, I won't fit into my clothes soon." Between Mazie's lavish meals and the times she'd eaten out over the past few days, she knew she'd already gained a few pounds. "And don't look so disappointed. You didn't honestly think I'd jump into bed with him, did you? We just met."

Bridgett raised a brow. "Him? Who him?"

"Clay him, that's who. We went to dinner the other night." Abby hoped her disappointment in not hearing from the man for the past forty hours didn't show. She certainly wasn't counting. Okay, she was. And Abby couldn't remember counting the hours on anything, except maybe when she was waiting for word to come down from the hospital board about her latest proposal.

Bridgett propped her elbows on the counter and leaned forward. "Clay Tanner…one of Hill Country's finest. I don't mean to pry, but I'm going to anyway. Why are you in Ramblewood? It must be something good if you hired a private investigator."

"It's no secret." Abby sipped her coffee. "According to my late biological father, I have a sister no one else apparently knows about. Since he was stationed at Randolph Air Force Base and I was born here, I figured I would try Texas first."

"I love mysteries," Bridgett said. "Any idea of her age?"

"No. I want to say younger than me, since he and my mom married straight out of high school, but who knows? Maybe he had an affair when he was overseas. I needed some place to start and Ramblewood was my jumping-off point."

"Let me know if there's anything I can do to help." Sympathy clouded Bridgett's eyes. "I don't know what I'd do if I were in your shoes."

Abby hoped that, whoever her sister turned out to be, she had as full and content a life as Abby did. Unless you counted the recent upset at work, age thirty creeping up in a few years, the lack of a boyfriend and a biological clock that was ticking louder with each of her friends' baby showers.

Okay. If she admitted the truth to herself, she wasn't as content as she wanted to be. But who was? Didn't people perpetually want more out of life? New cars, bigger houses, children. The grass was always greener.

"Mazie said Clay hadn't dated anyone since he moved back to town. That seems a little odd. What's his story?" Abby asked.

"That's the million dollar question, hon." Bridgett totaled up a customer's bill and tore the ticket from her pad. "The man who left for the ATF was not the same man who came home. All I can figure is something bad must've happened when he was working the Mexican border. He has a small ranch on the outskirts of town, but no one ever goes there. Either he's at Slater's Mill or Bridle Dance visiting Shane and Lexi, Mazie's sister. They have a house out there. Shane is Clay's best friend and even he doesn't know much. Or if he does, he hasn't said anything."

"Interesting," Abby commented.

"He's a tough one, Abby," Bridgett warned. "If you test the waters with him, I suggest you put on a life vest to keep your head above water. Someone like that can drag you down if you're not careful."

Bridgett's comment surprised Abby, although she should heed her advice considering how long the waitress had known the man. Abby's job was to help people regain their lives. She wasn't programmed to walk away. If Bridgett was right and something had happened to

Clay, that would explain why he was no longer with the ATF. Far too young to retire, he just didn't seem to fit the classic post-traumatic stress disorder profile. Not that it was her area of expertise, but she worked with many service people recovering from a range of injuries from limb loss to paralysis.

Clay didn't have the haunted look in his eyes she'd seen in them. No, he was different, but with only a week and a half left in her vacation, there wasn't enough time for her to help. At dinner he had asked all the questions, leaving her knowing nothing about him. Then again, that was his job as a private investigator, and her job was not Clay Tanner.

CLAY OWED ABBY an apology for behaving like a first-class jerk the other night. While they walked back to the Bed & Biscuit, Abby had maintained a chipper attitude, but her bubbliness and energy had faded with each step. Of course that had been Clay's fault, since he had virtually shut her out once he'd read that fortune cookie. He'd immediately felt as if he betrayed Ana Rosa with his personal interest in Abby.

He had asked himself many times if Ana Rosa would want him to move on or if she damned him to hell for causing her death. As religious as she'd been, in his heart Clay honestly didn't know if she'd forgive something so heinous. If she had forgiven him for her death, there'd be none when it came to Paulo's—a brilliant six-year-old with his entire life ahead of him. The little boy had wanted to be an American fireman more than anything—a dream Clay had promised to help fulfill.

He had planned to tell Ana Rosa the truth about his identity once the sting operation ended. Everything she'd known about him, everything she'd fallen in love with, had been a lie. But the lies had been a vital part of his assignment. They'd been necessary to keep them safe— or so he had thought. Clay had sensed things were about to go terribly wrong with that operation, and if he had disobeyed orders and told Ana Rosa and Paulo the truth, they'd still be alive. Instead, he had watched them die. That guilt tore at him each and every day.

Clay wanted to avoid any non-business-related contact with Abby, but there he was, contemplating calling her to apologize. He pulled into his parents' driveway, then climbed out of the truck, figuring a good dose of home would do him some good. Nothing ever changed at the Tanner house. He always knew what to expect when he walked through the door.

"Morning, Mom." He let himself in the side entrance. "Something smells good in here."

"Have a seat, honey." Fern gave him a quick kiss on the cheek. "I'm making waffles and you're just in time. I hoped you were stopping by. We haven't seen you for the past few days."

"Translation," his father chimed in from the hall archway. "Your mother heard from the Ramblewood Caw & Cackle Society that you went out on a date the other night, and she's dying for you to tell her all about it. Heard she's a cute little thing."

Clay rolled his eyes. His mother was a romantic. She kept scrapbooks from her courtship with his father all the way through Clay's and his sister's school years. Fern carefully documented and preserved every family event in one of her many volumes.

"Well?" his mom asked.

Clay's muscles tensed. "It wasn't a date. I met a client for dinner to discuss her case."

"Charlotte Hargrove said you two were walking down Main Street practically hand in hand," his mother said.

"Charlotte Hargrove needs a life of her own because I assure you Abby and I weren't holding hands." Clay roughly pulled out a chair and flopped onto it. "By the end of the night, she was barely speaking to me."

"What did you do?" Fern placed one hand on her hip and waved a spatula with the other. "You really need to stop running women off and start thinking about settling down. I want grandbabies and your sister, Hannah, vows never to have any. You're my only hope." She looked at her husband. "Right, Gage?"

"Fern, give the man a break," his dad said. "But I'm curious, what did you do to make her stop talking to you? Give a man some pointers, will you?"

His mother threw her dish towel at his father. They made marriage appear so effortless, and Clay couldn't get through a meal with a woman without ruining things.

After breakfast, he drove halfway home before calling Abby. He owed her an apology. That was it, nothing more. Yet he ended up asking her to meet him at Slater's Mill later that evening.

Why was he doing this to himself—to her? It wasn't fair to either one of them. He needed to find her sister quickly so Abby could leave town. *Keep telling yourself that, pal.* Yep, that's why he'd already spoken with Shane and planned to introduce Abby to some of the Langtrys tonight so she could hear about their hippotherapy facility and possibly want to stay in Ramblewood. Clay was baiting her, because whether he chose to admit it or not, he wanted Abby in his life.

THE PARKING LOT at Slater's Mill was half full when Clay arrived. He parked his truck and checked his reflection in the mirror, gently removing a piece of tissue from his face. In his haste to shower and shave he had nicked his chin. Stupid disposables—a rechargeable razor was his whisker-weapon of choice, but he still hadn't replaced the one he'd dropped on the bathroom floor last week.

A red-and-white Mini Cooper pulled in alongside him as he stepped from his truck. It must be Abby's—it suited her personality perfectly. He laughed. His midnight-blue Dodge Ram dwarfed her car. Clay adjusted his summer Stetson, checked his belt buckle to make sure he hadn't left anything open and ran his palms down the front of his jeans, kicking himself for being as nervous as a fly in a glue pot. He would introduce her to the Langtrys and they'd have one drink. A drink with a woman he found attractive and who filled his every thought.

Abby stepped out of her car. "You look great." The words unexpectedly escaped his mouth.

She grinned. "You're not too shabby yourself."

"I'm sorry again about the other night." Clay jammed his hands in his pockets and met her eyes. "That fortune cookie reminded me of someone and I let my emotions get the best of me. I hope you can accept my apology."

Abby nodded. "I figured it was something like that. I'm here, aren't I? So don't waste another minute worrying about it."

"After we spoke earlier I heard back from an associate of mine who was able to pull your father's military records. Unfortunately, there was no mention of another daughter, but did you know you're listed as the beneficiary on one of his IRA accounts?"

"No." Abby stared up at him in confusion. "I didn't know—I didn't think—"

"It's not enough to live on, but it's a nice amount." Clay understood her bewilderment. It wasn't the first time he'd told someone a loved one had left them money after they'd died. "I didn't bring the information with me tonight, but I'll get it to you tomorrow."

Abby blinked rapidly. "Okay." For a moment, Clay thought she was on the verge of tears, until he watched her take a deep breath, square her shoulders and smile. In that instant, she reminded him of himself when he was trying to keep it together. She flicked a thumb at the barnlike bar. "Shall we?" She strode ahead a few steps.

Long fringe ran down the back of Abby's ultra-high-heeled boots, swaying when she walked across the pavement. With the sorry state of the parking lot, she could break her neck in those things.

After her first wobble, Abby wound her arm tightly around Clay's, allowing him to escort her to the front door. Even in heels, she was almost a foot shorter than he was. Clay tried to match the swift strides of her toned legs. She might be vertically challenged, but it sure didn't slow her down.

Abby stopped shy of the door and adjusted the belt on her denim shirt dress. She tousled her long blond waves in the most innocent yet seductive way, smiled sweetly up at him and gripped his arm again.

Lord, have mercy.

"Show me how they do it in Texas, cowboy."

Clay swung the doors open and he led her in, proud she was by his side. "Oh!" Abby clapped. "I love this song. Dance with me!"

She didn't give him a chance to respond. She grabbed his hand and they tush-pushed their way to the center of the room and joined in the middle of a line dance. Matching Clay step for step, she maneuvered, turned and stomped like a pro.

"You're pretty good," Clay said midclap.

"I love to dance." Abby added an extra bit of flair to her turn. "I take a class every day back home."

"Every day?"

"Some people run, some bike ride, I dance."

The song ended and everyone in the room applauded. Clay pointed to a circular booth at the far end of the dance floor. "There are a couple of friends I'd like you to meet."

He led her across the dance floor to where Shane, Lexi, Bridgett and Shane's younger brother, Chase, sat, noting the way Abby made physical contact with everyone he introduced her to, with a touch on the shoulder or a handshake. The gestures were subtle yet personal. She gave each person her full attention. Clay imagined she was extremely attentive with her patients.

Abby tugged Clay onto the dance floor for another round. As soon as their boots hit the scuffed wood planks, the band began playing a slow song. Without hesitation, Abby wrapped her arms around Clay's neck. The immediate intimacy caused him to freeze. Fearing she would sense his hesitation, he placed his hands on her hips and swayed along to the music, probably more like a mule in clogs than a man who had been to more barn dances than he could count.

Abby pressed tightly against him and Clay prayed his body wouldn't betray his attraction. The scent of her hair reminded him of the field of bluebonnets next to his house on a spring morning. He slipped his hands farther around her, surprisingly grateful when the band played another country ballad. He gave Elvis Watts, the band's lead singer, an appreciative nod. Elvis gave him a thumbs-up in return.

"Thank you for this—for tonight." Abby pulled away slightly to look up at him, her smile melting his defenses.

"I can't remember the last time I actually relaxed and had a good time."

Truth be told, neither could he.

The dim light of the dance floor darkened her eyes to a sensuous inky blue. Her pupils dilated. Clay's voice caught in his throat and he swallowed hard.

"You're welcome" was all he could muster.

Regrettably—or fortunately, he wasn't sure which—the song ended and Clay led Abby back to their table as the band took an intermission. He ordered another round for everyone while Abby excused herself to go to the bathroom with Bridgett in tow, leaving him to stare after her like a lovestruck calf.

"What's the matter, old man?" Shane slapped him on the back. "Looks like you have your hands full with that one. See I was right, she's hot."

"Hey, now," Lexi said. "Don't forget I'm still sitting here."

"She's just a client," Clay said, "but I agree, she's blessed in the beauty department. And, there's no grass growing under her feet, that's for sure. She wore me out." He dropped into the booth next to Lexi and playfully tugged her hair. "Why aren't you up there tonight? Figured you'd be belting out a song or two."

Lexi lifted the side of her shirt to show him a large bruise on her left ribs.

"A horse got the best of me today." She lowered her shirt. "Knocked me clear across the stall with one kick."

One of the hazards of being an equine veterinarian, Lexi took the occasional tumble. And, like her sister Mazie, both were married to their jobs.

"Did you get X-rayed this time?" Stubborn as she was tough, Lexi was known for letting her own health play second fiddle to her four-legged patients. A few years ago, she had punctured a lung when a wayward rib shifted because she had refused to go to the hospital after a horse kicked her while she was tending its rattlesnake bitten leg. Lexi wouldn't consider risking an animal's life just because she was in pain, and her dedication made her one of the state's most respected equine vets.

"Aw, aren't you sweet. Worrying about little old me." Lexi half-heartedly smiled. "I was given a clean bill of health. I'm just sore. I'm hoping this bourbon here will make it all better."

Abby returned to the table and slid into the booth next to Bridgett, forcing Clay to pull up a chair and sit out in the open. A part of him preferred to sit thigh to thigh with her, but this way was safer. Or not. When she shifted, he realized his vantage point gave him full view of her shapely bare legs. *So much for safe.* He hadn't considered himself a leg man before, but he seemed unable to resist hers.

"I hear you're a physical therapist," Chase said. "You're more than welcome to come out to our ranch anytime."

Abby smiled. "Thanks. I met your mother the other day. Clay tells me she runs a hippotherapy facility. Is she a therapist?"

"No, she's the CEO. Dance of Hope was our father's baby, but he died before it came to fruition," Chase said over the music. "We had the grand opening last year, alongside our Ride 'em High! Rodeo School. The two facilities share an enclosed arena, with a couple of separate outdoor rodeo arenas in front and private hippotherapy corrals in the back."

"My condolences on your father's death." Abby leaned over the table so she wouldn't have to yell, causing her hair to brush against Clay's arm. A slight shiver coursed through his body and he silently cursed the effect she had on him. "Are you sure your mom wouldn't mind my stopping in without any advance warning?"

"Not at all," Shane said. "She'd love to show you around. Clay said you have a therapy dog. Feel free to bring him along."

Abby gave Clay a look that told him she was surprised that his friends knew so much about her. He guessed he had built her up quite a bit when he'd called Shane and asked them to meet him and Abby tonight.

"I will," she said. "Thanks. I'm still in awe of the effect therapy animals have on people." Clay sat back and admired the passion in Abby's voice when she spoke. "I was reviewing some case studies last night. One involved a bone marrow transplant patient who had retreated into his shell. It was a battle when it came to his physical therapy. Eventually, he became unresponsive. When they added a dog to the patient's therapy, the man's spirits and physical well-being changed dramatically. Mundane little things such as petting a dog improve body movement. Throwing a ball increases range of motion and helps rebuild muscles."

"I wish you could've met our father," Chase said. "You share his passion for animal-assisted therapy. His was horse related, but the concept is very much the same."

"It would have been an honor to know him," Abby said. "It's amazing how animals can aid in both mental and physical recovery." She directed her attention to Lexi. "What do you do?"

"I'm an equine vet by day, his wife by night." Lexi playfully nudged Shane.

Clay wished he could say the instant rapport Abby developed with everyone surprised him. There was a definite connection between her and this town, and it went way beyond just being her birthplace. She seamlessly fit in with everyone at the table, and Clay had a suspicion that once Abby saw Dance of Hope the sheer magnitude of the facility and the services they offered would leave her wanting to be a part of it.

Abby's enthusiasm rose with every animal therapy case she shared. Her genuine love of working with people and improving their quality of life was evident with each word she spoke. Clay watched Shane tug Lexi closer to give her a kiss. He pictured Abby tucked under his arm in the same way. No woman had captivated him so quickly before. Not even—

An announcement for karaoke interrupted his thoughts. Abby looked around the table, then shrugged.

"Excuse me." She stood and straightened her dress. "If none of you are going up, then I will. I find karaoke next to impossible to resist."

The audience on the dance floor erupted when Abby stepped in front of the microphone, drowning out any further conversation. The woman knew how to attract attention. A Miranda Lambert song played and Abby belted out the words as if she'd written them herself. The woman could sing!

Clay scanned the various women on the dance floor, trying to detect a resemblance to Abby. Four days into the case and he still didn't have any solid leads despite devoting more time to her search than any other client he had. The phrase "needle in a haystack" definitely applied here. He had begun to secretly hope that he'd discover her sister living in town, which would give Abby a reason to come back and visit. But the chances of that were next to none.

When the song ended, the room filled with whistles and shouts for more. Abby smiled at the crowd and met Clay's eyes, then motioned for him to join her. He protested until Shane and Chase pulled him to his feet. Being ushered on stage hadn't figured into his plans this evening, yet somehow he found himself prodded forward like a steer.

"Sing a duet with me." Abby directed him to the song list.

"Abby, I don't think—"

"Then don't. Have some fun and loosen up a little." She shimmied her shoulders side to side for emphasis.

"I'm loose." Clay shook his own shoulders, trying to emulate her. A few of the locals near the stage hooted and hollered at his dance move.

"Prove it!" Abby yelled above the noise.

"Move over." Clay hip-checked Abby out of the way. Perfume lingered in the air when she moved and he inhaled the scent deeper, committing it to memory. He couldn't believe he was on stage. The last time had probably been a good ten years ago. Abby made it easy to laugh and have fun, and Clay forced himself to focus on the song list so he could prove to her he wasn't uptight.

The music started. Abby cocked her head and looked upward, trying to figure out the tune. She nodded to the beat and smiled. The words to "Picture," a duet by Kid Rock and Sheryl Crow, appeared on the screen and Abby sang her part without having to cheat and look at the lyrics. Only she didn't merely sing...she performed.

Not to be outdone, when it was his turn Clay stepped in front of her and belted out his part. Then she did the same. Each time their turn came up, they tried to upstage the other. Clay felt as if he was in a comedy routine. Finally, he gave up and stood behind her, resting his hands and chin on the top of her head.

When the song ended, Abby threw herself into Clay's arms. He spun her around, feeling freer than he had in years. She was inches from his face and her lips parted when their eyes met. He closed his for a moment and that was all it took for Clay to forget where they were.

His lips crashed down upon hers, pent-up frustration colliding with his desire for the one woman who had managed to turn his head for the first time in years. He held her in his arms, her body pressed against his so close, he could have sworn their hearts beat in unison.

Whoops and howls from the crowd filtered into his brain, quickly bringing him back to reality. He had kissed Abby in front of half the town. He released her abruptly. Her mouth fell open, then snapped shut before she hopped off stage with the assistance of some people in the front row, leaving Clay to stand in the spotlight alone.

WHAT THE HELL WAS THAT? The last thing Abby had expected tonight was a kiss, especially one on stage in front of Clay's friends and practically the entire town. She'd seen regret on his face the instant he broke the kiss, ruining the moment. The kiss had been amazing, though. He wanted her. No doubt about it.

Sliding into the booth next to Bridgett, Abby was glad everyone else was on the dance floor. "Don't say it."

"Don't say what?" Bridgett took a swallow of beer. "You're old enough to make your own decisions. Just make sure there's water in the pool before you jump in."

"Did you see the look on his face?" Abby wasn't one to shy away from a man, but when he suddenly released her in front of everyone, she'd wanted to crawl into a hole.

Bridgett shook her head. "He had his back to us. Your face said enough."

"Do you think if I hid under the table anyone would miss me?"

"Do you really want to know what I think?" Bridgett set her bottle on the table.

"Go for it." Abby braced herself for an onslaught.

"I think everyone was surprised to see Clay walk in here with you. They were even more surprised when he got up on that stage and sang. That was the old Clay we haven't seen in years."

"Really?" Clay had seemed so natural singing next to her.

"Yep, the kiss was a bonus. Congratulations for breaking through part of his armor." Bridgett raised her bottle to Abby. "But, before you run off and celebrate…the way he abruptly ended it? Well, that's the typical brooding Clay we've become accustomed to since he returned. I promise, no one thinks any less of you. Clay, on the other hand, looked like an ass for potentially blowing the best thing that ever happened to him." Bridgett smiled. "Abby, it's his loss, not yours."

Abby watched Clay talk to an older man at the bar. He didn't once look her way. Their kiss, however brief, had contained real emotion, and Abby wished she knew if Clay had backed away out of fear or because he'd been caught up in the moment. Fear she could handle. People overcame fear with a little work. Regret…that was a different story, especially if something or someone from his past was stopping him from moving forward with his life.

Questions beckoned, and she was determined to find the answers, including the one surrounding Clay's heart.

FOR AN HOUR, he'd forgotten about the past. Forgotten he even *had* a past. But now? Guilt weighed heavy in his heart. Had he betrayed Ana Rosa's memory by kissing Abby? His fiancée was gone. He'd never feel her soft skin against his again. He'd never hear her say *I love you* in her horrible Americanized accent. The woman had had so much heart, determined to learn English from him and Paulo so she'd fit in better with Clay's family.

Family...some days he cursed the word. He had figured they'd have had kids of their own by now, and it would have been Ana Rosa by his side tonight. That was the way it was supposed to be, and it would have been if he hadn't made the biggest mistake of his life and cost them theirs.

Abby tested his devotion to Ana Rosa's memory each time he was with her. He knew he was in love with the memory of what was, but he wasn't ready to move on. Not yet.

Not wanting to head back to the table and face Abby, Clay ordered another beer. Beau Bradley, one of Ramblewood's old-timers, sat at the far end, talking with one of his cronies. Clay joined them. There'd be no heavy conversations among these men. He needed a safe zone.

"Scoping out the ladies, tonight?" Clay slapped the older man on the shoulder.

"I see you caught yourself a little something." Beau motioned across the dance floor with his beer bottle in Abby's direction.

"She's actually a client," Clay said. If anyone knew old Ramblewood gossip, it was Beau. "But I have a feeling you already knew that."

"Yep, word travels fast in these parts." Beau tapped his feet to the beat of the music and swigged his beer. "Since when do you kiss your clients on stage?"

Clay ignored the comment. "She's looking for her long-lost sister and thinks someone in Ramblewood might remember her parents or have some sort of information we can use." Beau took a longer tug on his beer than usual. "You wouldn't happen to know anything, would you?"

Beau's hand hesitated slightly as he set his bottle on the bar top.

"Can we talk?" Abby tapped his shoulder. Clay turned around. Her small smile held a touch of sadness. Her confusion over their kiss probably matched his own. "Just give me one minute."

When Clay turned back around to the bar, Beau was gone.

Chapter Four

Abby tossed and turned most of the night. What was up with Clay? The question attacked her mind for hours. He had mumbled something about needing to find a man who had just left the bar, then he'd torn out of Slater's Mill. She hadn't had a chance to talk to him about their very public display of affection. It hadn't been the most gentle of kisses, but it definitely ranked as the most passionate one she'd ever experienced. At the moment she felt like Georgie Porgie from the old nursery rhyme, only *she* had kissed the boy and made him cry...and then he'd run away. Nothing screamed *desperate* like a stranger kissing the resident bachelor in front of half the town. How could she have done something so stupid?

Abby willed herself out of bed and dressed. It was a new day, with a new set of possibilities. After Duffy's morning visit to the Bark Park, Abby decided to pop across the street to the Curl Up & Dye Salon for a much needed mani-pedi. A little pampering always managed to brighten her day. Well, that and new yarn. Earlier, Mazie had told Abby about the Knitter's Circle a block away, but they didn't open until eleven. She wanted some girlie distraction from the thoughts churning in her head... knitting and manicures fit the bill. Throw in a cupcake and she'd be in heaven.

Abby blinked as she pushed open the door of the salon. She wasn't quite sure what she had expected by way of decor in the salon, but the pink giraffe-print ceiling was a definite surprise. Dozens of large round mirrors hung on sherbet-striped walls that contrasted with the stark white tile floor. The rest of town had a *Happy Days* meets *The Waltons* vibe going on, and she had assumed the salon would be more of the same. Instead, it was elegantly eclectic, with just a touch of flamboyance carefully balanced with the sophistication of the sleek black styling chairs and *très chic* frosted-glass manicure stations.

"Hello, I'm Kylie," trilled the woman who greeted her at the door, almost knocking Abby back onto the street with her high-pitched voice and overly sweet perfume. "Welcome to Curl Up and Dye, where we beautify until you're satisfied."

Seriously?

Abby fought the grin threatening to betray her thoughts. The woman had said only a couple of words— albeit they were a mouthful—but it was Kylie's wide-eyed, simple expression, complete with head tilt, that almost made Abby snicker. Fitted, black ponte-pants and a body-hugging pink T-shirt flawlessly coordinated with the twentysomething's pink-and-black French manicure. While her long, layered, chocolate-hued tresses were a bit on the voluminous side, they had the most incredible sheen. Kylie was beautiful in every sense of the word, but her aura definitely screamed *space cadet*.

"Hi, I'm Abby and I'm new in—"

"I know who you are." Kylie giggled, practically bubbling over with excitement. "You're the talk of Ramblewood."

"I'm the what?"

"You made out with Clay at Slater's last night." Kylie

leaned closer and whispered. "And from where I stood, it looked like a *romp-tastic* kiss. If only Aaron would kiss me like that." Kylie dramatically patted her heart.

Oh, my stars, the woman has little black rhinestone bow-ties on the tips of her fingernails. Abby rubbed her forehead, trying to focus on Kylie's words.

"Who's Aaron? And it really wasn't that big of a deal."

Okay, so it was a kiss. And while it lasted all of five seconds, it didn't come anywhere close to what Abby would call making out. As good as it had been, she wasn't quite sure it fit into the *romp-tastic* category, either. Regardless, it had caught Kylie's attention and apparently the rest of the town's, too.

"Aaron's my beau. Has been for years." Kylie twirled a strand of hair before she tucked it behind her ear and made certain nobody else was listening. "Between you and me, I don't think I'm ever going to be anything more than his girlfriend. I'd like to get hitched at some point, and while the man can shake the rafters loose in the bunkhouse a couple of times a night, he stays in the shadows of his momma's apron when it comes to the *'til death do us part* department, if you know what I mean."

Was she really having this conversation with a complete stranger? "Um, I'm sure your day will come. I don't know the guy, but if it's true love, he'll ask you at some point."

"I guess—but hey, enough about me." Kylie lowered her voice again. "Tell me, what was it like kissing one of Ramblewood's hottest bachelors? I swear you made every single girl in town jealous."

Abby had no idea kissing Clay would knock the earth off its axis. "It was one kiss."

"Yes, but it was Clay Tanner. No one kisses the P.I. No woman can get close enough."

"So I've been told."

"Whatever you've done, keep doing it. You bring out a side of Clay we haven't seen in a long time. Can I just tell you, when I was fifteen, I had the biggest crush on him you could imagine."

Maybe a trip to the salon was a huge mistake. Abby peeked at her watch trying to come up with an excuse to escape.

"I'd love to stay and chat all day, but I just remembered—"

"Of course, I'm so sorry. You're just so easy to talk to." Kylie's voice changed pitch so many times Abby thought her eardrums would burst. "I'm sure you didn't come in here to listen to me babble, so what can we do for you?"

"I'd like a mani-pedi." Abby didn't see anyone at the manicure stations. "Is it possible to get one or am I here too early?"

"Luna's on the schedule today, but she hasn't come in yet. Ruby—she's the owner—will probably do it for you."

Before Abby could object, Kylie disappeared through a door at the back of the salon. *What have I gotten myself into?* She had entered *The Twilight Zone.*

A woman whose candy-apple-red hair was pulled back into a modern bouffant on top, with the remaining hair cascading over her shoulders, appeared alongside Kylie. The woman had a slight limp and winced with each step. Either she was in pain or her black leather pants were a tad too tight.

"It's so wonderful to meet you!" The woman hugged Abby hard. "I'm Ruby. My daughter, Bridgett, has told me quite a lot about you."

"Oh, wow, you're Bridgett's mom." Abby tried to recover from the unexpected welcome. Somehow, she had pictured Bridgett's mother to be more *Leave It to Beaver* than *Whisky a Go-Go*. For a woman probably nearing her fifties, she looked at least ten years younger. "It's a pleasure to meet you. I can come back for a manicure when—Luna, is it?—gets in. I didn't mean to pull you away from anything."

"You didn't, and I don't mind one bit." Ruby stepped behind one of the glass tables and gingerly lowered herself into the chair. "Do you want a pedicure? I have the time."

"I had planned on it, but I'm going to the Bridle Dance Ranch a little later, and I think sneakers are a better choice than sandals. I'm afraid my toes won't have a chance to fully dry by then."

"Gorgeous place and the Langtrys are real *gen-u-ine* people, you know?" Ruby's Southern accent was thick and definitely had more twang than Bridgett's. Or anyone else's she'd met in town so far. Definitely not a Ramblewood native. "Let's remove your polish and soak those cuticles. You want me to keep them short or would you like some gel tips?"

"Short. I work with my hands and long nails get in the way." Abby admired Ruby's long red-and-white plaid embellished nails. "I love yours, though. Are you able to do that design on mine?"

"Sure thing, hon."

After a quick soak in what smelled vaguely of honey and dish soap, the woman filed Abby's nails. Sensing Ruby studying her, Abby shifted in her seat. Why is it people hated to catch someone in the act of staring at them? Abby braved a glance and Ruby smiled back, never missing a stroke of the emery board.

"Bridgett tells me you're in town looking for your sister." Ruby didn't break eye contact.

Abby cleared her throat, grateful for the icebreaker,

but uneasy with the woman who gripped her hand. There was something unsettling about Ruby, but Abby couldn't place what it was. Where she had no problem discussing her search with Janie, she didn't feel the same with Ruby. Thankful she had passed on the pedicure, Abby wished she had skipped the salon altogether.

"I don't have much to go on, so it may be a lost cause in the end." Abby wanted to steer the conversation onto a less personal subject. "In the meantime, I'm excited to visit the Dance of Hope Hippotherapy Center at the Langtry's ranch. Have you been there?"

"I went to their ribbon cutting last year." Ruby grinned as she applied a base coat to Abby's nails. "It's an interesting place, and I hear they do good things for people, but wouldn't you like to see more of the sights while you're in town? Ramblewood is nice and all, but San Antonio is only about an hour away. I'm sure Bridgett wouldn't mind going along with you."

"I appreciate the sentiment, but my interest in Dance of Hope is professional. I'm a physical therapist and I want to see how their program works. I've read about hippotherapy and I understand the concept of how the horse's movements mimic those of a human are used to treat people with disabilities and injuries, but I've never seen it in action. It absolutely fascinates me, and I'd love to learn how they combine horses and physical therapy. The hospital where I work doesn't have any animal-assisted programs, and it doesn't look like they will any time in the future, either."

"Then maybe Ramblewood's a good fit for you." Ruby rolled a bottle of red polish between her hands.

"It's a temporary fit." The truth of the matter was that she had already begun to feel how perfect Ramblewood was for her. "My life is back home in Charleston, South Carolina."

"Never say never, dear. Kylie tells me you already found yourself a man. Who knows, maybe you'll find your true happiness here."

"They weren't kidding about small-town gossip, were they?" Abby jerked her head up at Ruby's words. Sure, she was getting used to the Clay thing, but she hadn't experienced the happiness part in years. Lately, it seemed everything she tried to accomplish was a battle, and instead of heeding the advice she gave her patients—seek out happiness—she constantly wrestled with the growing resentment she felt regarding the closed-mindedness of those around her, her family included. Wyatt, especially, since he'd made her feel awkward in her own home this past month. If Abby wanted to grieve, she should be able to do so without someone berating her about why she felt anything for a man she barely knew.

"Excuse me for being too personal." Abby directed her attention to Ruby's face. Flamboyant hair and attire aside, there was a softness to the woman she hadn't noticed at first glance. And why shouldn't she get personal? The woman clearly took the liberty of injecting herself into Abby's life, so she was only returning the favor. "I noticed earlier that you seem to have some pain on your left side."

"I broke my leg a couple years ago, thanks to that one over there." Ruby nodded in Kylie's direction.

"I'm Ruby's indentured servant." Kylie's tone was sharp. "I spilled some shampoo on the floor, and before I had a chance to clean it up Ruby slipped and fell. She's never let me live it down."

"As I was saying…" Ruby glanced sideways at Kylie before returning her attention to Abby. "I went through some physical therapy until my insurance ran out, but my leg never felt right, even though the doctors said it healed fine. Some days are worse than others. Today is one of those days. I'm feeling a little off balance. I wouldn't be able to stand at one of those stations and cut hair, that's for sure. Sitting is better. Not great, but better. It's just something I have to live with."

"No, Ruby, you shouldn't have to live with it." Abby thought the woman was a bit eccentric, but she couldn't turn away from someone she might be able to help. "I'd be happy to give you a full evaluation, no charge, so don't worry about paying me. Don't sell yourself short and think you have to live with the pain."

"If you're sure it wouldn't be too much trouble." Ruby's face brightened. "I'd love some relief. I'm not one of those people who swallow a pill whenever they get a hangnail. And I'll give you free salon treatments the entire time you're in town."

"It's a deal. We'll try a few different exercises and see if we can begin to get you back to feeling like yourself again. I can't make any promises, but I'd be more than happy to meet with you later today when I return from Dance of Hope."

"You're a remarkable young woman," Ruby said. "So accomplished and caring. Your parents must be proud."

"I'd like to think they are." Abby watched Ruby stroke color onto her nails. Fifteen minutes ago she had wanted to escape the salon. Now she was actually enjoying herself. Ruby wasn't so bad. The way everyone made her feel welcome almost felt more like home than Charleston currently did. But maybe that was only natural, since Ramblewood is where everything had begun.

GUILT COUPLED WITH DESIRE had kept Clay awake all night. Now that he had kissed Abby, she was ingrained in his every thought. As if she hadn't been before. It seemed worse today.

But Clay had a job to do. He wasn't just searching for Abby's sister, he had other clients to work for, as well. He had employment verifications to run, a report to compile for an insurance company on a disability fraud case and a ton of background checks to conduct for a new dating service company in San Antonio. He needed to concentrate, not pine over some woman who was leaving in a little over a week.

Clay sat at his kitchen table and flipped open his laptop. Even with the blinds still closed, he could see the stacks of boxes beckoning him from the darkened dining room. They taunted him today.

He was tired of the ache that constantly plagued him. He hadn't realized it until he spent time with Abby. Her lightness was good...healthy compared to his perpetual heartache. But he didn't know how to move on from Ana Rosa. He'd met with a government-appointed psychiatrist until it was no longer mandatory, but nothing they'd discussed eased his conscience.

He glanced around his house. This wasn't what Clay wanted...working out of the kitchen with the rest of the house dark so he wouldn't have to face the reality of what his life had become. How did a person let go of someone they had loved so intensely and still did to this day?

Clay rubbed his temples. It was much different when a relationship simply ended. Death was harder. Final. When Ana Rosa had died, a part of his heart had died with her. Clay hadn't thought any woman could make his heart beat again. But Abby had from the moment they had met. He ran a hand along his jaw. Clay refused to fall for her further. He wasn't sure he could handle any relationship, and a long-distance one was out of the question.

He needed to get out of the house for a while. What he really needed was an office somewhere, but that would have to wait until he cleared his schedule a bit. He glanced at the file folder sitting on the chair next to him. It contained the background check on one of the new accountants Cole Langtry wanted to hire. It would be easier if he emailed it over as he usually did, but Clay could use the change of scenery. Grabbing his laptop, he decided that working anywhere else was better than working from home today.

The tension eased from Clay's shoulders once he pulled past the rearing bronze horse statues at the entrance of the Langtry ranch. Bridle Dance had always been his home away from home. Pecan trees heavy with fruit formed an arch over the dirt road. In another couple of weeks or so, the townsfolk would help shake the limbs with long paddled poles. In exchange for helping the Langtrys harvest the nuts, everyone received a ten-pound sack of pecans to take home. It was one more way Joe Langtry had brought Ramblewood together and the tradition continued after his death. Before they harvested the first pecan, everyone would join hands and remember the man so many missed.

Clay immediately spotted Abby's Mini Cooper near the indoor riding arena. *Great.* His shoulders tensed. She had wasted no time taking the Langtrys up on their offer. Hoping to avoid Abby, Clay ambled through the stables, or what Joe Langtry had referred to as his horse mansion. Rivaling the size of a football field, the French-stone and stucco building more than earned the title. Bridle Dance sat on a quarter of a million acres, and was one of the state's largest paint and quarter cutting horse ranches. They pampered their horses in every way possible.

Clay strolled down the exposed-timber interior hallway and then climbed the mahogany staircase leading to the second-story offices.

"Hey, man." Clay slapped Shane on the shoulder. "Is Cole around? I have that background check he asked for."

Clay didn't think he'd ever get used to seeing Shane sitting behind a mountain of paperwork. The former rodeo star had given up his life in the spotlight to run his rodeo school and to see his and Lexi's teenage son compete in the junior circuit.

"You know you could've emailed this to my brother, right?" Shane smiled. "I don't have to ask why you hand-delivered it considering she passed through here with my mother about ten minutes ago."

"Believe it or not, I came here so I wouldn't think about Abby. I was surprised to see her car when I pulled in." Clay walked to one of the large Craftsman-style windows encircling the room and peered out over the therapy corrals behind the indoor arena.

"What happened to you last night, anyway?" Shane asked. "One minute you were kissing her, the next you were gone. I have to hand it to her, though. You acted like a first-class ass and she remained smiling. She even got back on stage with Bridgett for a rendition of the Dixie Chicks' 'Ready to Run.'"

"'Ready to Run'? Really?" Clay bet everyone had had a good laugh at his expense. "That's embarrassing."

"For you, maybe," Shane said. "Although, as much as Abby tried to hide it, I think she was embarrassed herself."

"I didn't come here to be harassed," Clay snapped and crossed his arms over his chest.

"Hey, I get it. You don't want to be involved with some-one who isn't going to stick around. Say no more, but if you do happen to be interested, you'll find her in the hippotherapy center."

Nothing like a subtle push toward the person he wanted to avoid. Clay said goodbye to Shane and made his way back through the stables, stopping briefly to chat with some of the grooms. He wasn't sure if he was hoping to avoid running into Abby or if he was just in the mood to be over-friendly.

His relationship with Ana Rosa couldn't have been more different. He'd been extremely protective of her and Paulo because Ana Rosa's brother was one of the gunrunners he had been trying to take down, and the man kept a close watch on his sister. Ana Rosa had been in danger every time she had seen her brother, but Clay had been unable to warn her to stay away. Not when Clay was supposedly working for the man. Ana Rosa's vulnerability was a stark contrast to Abby's take-no-prisoners attitude.

Stepping outside, he spotted Kay and Abby leaning against the white fence surrounding the hippotherapy corrals. Cue the butterflies. Clay hated admitting Abby caused his stomach to flutter, because no man in his right mind liked butterflies.

"CLAY, HOW WONDERFUL to see you," Kay said. "I'm so glad you stopped by. I hear you and Abby are acquainted with each other."

Clearly the matriarch had heard about their kiss from her sons or even Abby directly. Regardless of what had happened, Clay held Kay personally responsible for pushing Abby in his direction.

No matter how hard he tried, he found himself staring straight into Abby's eyes. "I had a background check to drop off for Cole and I saw Abby's car when I pulled in. I thought I'd stop by and see how she was making out on her tour." Clay could have kicked himself. Out of all the things he could've said, he chose the one that made him look interested. He shouldn't be here. He needed to get into his truck and head back to his own ranch.

Abby's smile and the sudden pinkness of her cheeks made Clay almost turn to mud at her feet. Her smile was all it took. With her hair pulled back in a high ponytail and wearing a simple gray T-shirt, jeans and sneakers, she looked much more casual today. And much shorter. But what she lacked in height she made up for in curves. He preferred the sneakers over the four-inch heels.

Kay nudged Abby lightly with her elbow. Abby was clearly at a loss for words. Her silence was his fault—he had acted horribly after their kiss. But he didn't want to lead her on. Hell, he didn't want to lead himself on. His boots felt as though they were rooted in the dirt.

"So," Abby said. "Have you had any leads on my case?"

Case? She wanted to talk about her case? Clay blinked. Of course she did. After bailing on her a second time, he couldn't possibly expect her to think there was anything else between them. She had the right idea…keep it strictly professional and no hearts would get broken. Why did his disappointment feel worse than his nerves?

"Not yet. But I assure you I'm working diligently on it."

"I have an idea," Kay said. "It's almost lunchtime, so why don't you two join me up at the house, then afterward you can go riding and Clay can give you a tour of the ranch."

"Ride? You mean on horseback?" Abby asked hesitantly, looking from the corral to the stables.

"Have you ever been on a horse?" Kay asked.

Abby shook her head.

"Better yet…Clay has a Welsh pony at his place that

would fit you perfectly. I'm sure he'd be more than happy to give you some private lessons."

Clay bit down on the side of his tongue. Kay was matchmaking, all right. She was trying to push them together. And she wasn't shy about it, either.

"Sure." Clay struggled to maintain an even voice. "But if Abby's interested in hippotherapy, wouldn't she be better off experiencing a horse for the first time from a patient's perspective?"

Kay's eyes narrowed and Clay fought back a smile. He never thought the day would come where he'd best the woman at her own game.

"You're right, she would." Kay smirked. "After lunch, we'll get her on one of our ponies. By then, Ever will be home from school and she can help out." Kay turned to Abby. "Ever is my granddaughter. She has cerebral palsy, and hippotherapy took her from being wheelchair bound to being able to walk with only braces on her legs."

"I'd love to meet her." Abby watched one of the therapists work with a rider in the corral. "And Clay's correct. As a physical therapist I'd like to experience the same process a patient would. The things you do here are incredible. I knew you had the cottages for the long-term residents and their families and I knew how certain things worked from the videos you posted online, but to see it in person is amazing."

Abby wiped her cheek with shaky fingers. Her emotion touched Clay as they watched the riders.

"It's okay, dear." Kay rubbed Abby's back.

"I'm sorry." She attempted to laugh. "When I see someone making progress with their therapy, it sometimes overwhelms me. Especially when it involves animals. This is why I'm urging the hospital to consider nonconventional therapy."

Kay protectively wrapped an arm around Abby. "I know you have a job in Charleston and your dedication to your patients is remarkable, but if this is something you'd be interested in seriously pursuing, I can fit you in here. You'd have to get your PATH certification…meaning the Professional Association of Therapeutic Horsemanship, but I'd help you with that. Don't answer just yet. Mull it over and see how you feel about it."

Abby looked up at Kay, eyes wide. "I don't know what to say. Thank you. I don't see how I possibly could, but I'll consider it."

"Then tomorrow Clay can start giving you actual riding lessons since the saddle we use for hippotherapy is completely different than the tack you use to ride a horse for pleasure. If you're in Texas, riding is a must."

The woman didn't miss an opportunity. Clay was still trying to process Kay offering Abby a job and now she had promised riding lessons on his behalf.

"I—I don't want to impose on you, Clay," Abby stammered.

"You wouldn't be." Clay knew his heart had reached the danger zone.

"There you have it." Kay smiled, squeezed herself in between them and wrapped her arms around Clay and Abby, directing them toward the house. "Let's have lunch, and I won't take no for an answer."

Robotically, Clay walked with them. Regardless of how slight the chances were that Abby would accept Kay's offer, it was officially a real possibility. And that scared Clay to death.

Chapter Five

"I can't believe she offered me a job." Abby poured her third cup of coffee before daybreak. "She doesn't even know who I am."

"That's Kay Langtry and that's the way Joe lived his life and ran his business." Mazie bustled around the inn's kitchen preparing blueberry scones for breakfast. "I can't even begin to tell you how many people got second chances and new lives around this town because of the Langtrys."

"What time is it, anyway?" The last clock Abby had checked read four in the morning.

"I'm guessing it's almost five."

"I've heard of waking up with the chickens, but you're up way before they are. Are you always in the kitchen this early?"

"Usually. I don't require much sleep. I like to offer my guests a good breakfast. I don't go all out like I do for a dinner, but I like fresh breads, scones and croissants… and those things take time."

"You're the Martha Stewart of Texas." Abby laughed.

"You sound like Lexi. My sister's always ragging on me, but you've never seen more of a workaholic than that one. Well, she was until she got married last year. I never thought I'd see the day that the wild and rebellious Lexi

Lawson would settle down. She was definitely voted least likely to tie the knot around here. Speaking of romance, what's going on with you and the P.I.?"

"He's giving me a riding lesson this morning," Abby said over her coffee. "I'm excited. Yesterday was my first time on a horse and it was amazing. The therapists at Dance of Hope are unbelievable. Everyone works together as a team and after meeting some of the long-term patients, I'm even more impressed with the facility. I know it's foolish even to consider Kay's offer, but she asked me to think it over. In the meantime, I thought I'd make the most of my trip and learn all I can about horses."

"Whose idea was it for Clay to become your personal trainer?" Mazie stilled the wooden spoon in her mixing bowl and faced Abby. "I'd think the best way for you to learn would be at Bridle Dance, where you could split your time between Dance of Hope and working with one of the grooms in the main stables."

"It was Kay's idea," Abby admitted.

"She's certainly become the busy matchmaker."

Abby tensed at Mazie's clipped tone. "Are you interested in Clay?"

Mazie almost dropped her bowl. "God, no. Trust me, I have absolutely no interest in Clay. I had my big romance with a pastry instructor in Paris—it came, it went and I will probably never experience anything close to it again. Clay's been pretty closed off since he came back to town. Lexi told me he had his heart broken when he was in the ATF, and whoever the woman was, it had a profound effect on him. I don't know if you plan to keep this little romance you two have going long distance or if you plan to continue it if you do move here, but just keep your eyes open with Clay."

"There's no romance. We shared one kiss and I doubt it will be repeated." Especially since Kay had foisted her on the man. Friendship, on the other hand, that was a possibility.

Mazie joined Abby at the table. "Why do you want to leave Charleston? I thought you were determined to see this animal therapy thing through at your hospital."

"I don't want to leave. I have a great job that pays very well and an incredible benefits package I'd hate to lose. My patients can be difficult, but understandably so. They usually have long journeys ahead of them and it's my job to see them through it." She clasped her hands together. "While the hospital and I don't agree on the AAT program, my job's not in any danger. Honestly, I've put in too much time there to walk away for something I know very little about. I don't even know if I could swing it financially. Between all the training I'd have to do, I probably wouldn't earn a salary for a while, never mind the expenses on the house my brother and I share." She sighed. "Once I do pull a salary, I'm sure it won't be anything close to what I make at the hospital, considering Dance of Hope is a nonprofit."

"Sounds like you've already decided," Mazie said. "Hippotherapy is very different from the therapy you want to introduce into the hospital."

Abby sipped her coffee. "I can't even begin to tell you what it was like to see those therapy animals at work on a scale as grand as an equine facility." She set her cup on the table. "I'd heard of PATH International before, but other than their name, I didn't know much about them. I'll admit, hippotherapy does fascinate me. The sheer fact that the rhythmic movements of the horse are used as a treatment for a variety of disorders from head and spine injuries to scoliosis is an opportunity I almost feel foolish to pass up."

"I wish you could see your face right now," Mazie tittered. "You're positively beaming."

Abby touched her cheeks. "When I sat on that horse, I gained a new perspective about what therapy patients feel and see. It was my first time on a horse, as I'm sure it is for many patients, and that alone was scary. But then you had the whole process. The thin fabric saddle allowed me to feel the horse beneath me. And even though I had two large handles to hold on to and assistants on either side of me, I was still scared. But Gracie—she was the physical therapist who showed me how a typical session works—was able to relax me so I could focus on the horse. It blew me away." She clapped her hands. "And then I actually saw a patient in town! Based on what I witnessed with her and the research I've done, she might be a good candidate for hippotherapy. I need to consult with Dance of Hope, of course, but it was great to know that option is available for the woman."

"You know, there's no harm in making a pros-and-cons list and see where it leads you." Mazie stood and lined a cookie sheet with parchment paper. "You'd better go get ready to meet Clay. I'll fix you a picnic breakfast to take with you. I'm sure he'll appreciate it. The man has his hands full on that ranch by himself, and he'll be champing at the bit to get started this morning."

Abby bounded up the first few steps before she remembered the early hour. Not wanting to wake the other guests, she tiptoed the rest of the way. She closed the door to her room, then grabbed her robe and padded into the bathroom. As she stared at herself in the mirror, she once again wondered if her sister looked anything like her. "Walter, I need more of a clue. Am I even in the right place?"

Immediately, her thoughts turned to Clay. He was the one person who could provide the answers, if only he could find the key. There was more going on here than just a missing sister. If Ramblewood was the right place, Walter would have known about Dance of Hope. Abby had discussed the hospital's rejections with him, and he knew how much an AAT program meant to her. But he couldn't possibly have known about Clay...could he? The man was the only private investigator in town.

"This is crazy." Abby turned on the shower and stepped under the water. "There's no possible way he could have known."

CLAY WAS SURPRISED to see Abby's Mini Cooper maneuver down his dirt driveway near the barn. Granted, he had told her she could come over for a riding lesson, but he hadn't thought it would be this early. He wanted to try to locate Beau again this morning and discover why the man had skipped out on him so abruptly the other night at Slater's Mill.

Abby waved through the windshield. She stepped out and leaned on the open-windowed door. "I should've called first. I'm sorry, I didn't even think. Is this an okay time?"

"Sure. I didn't think you city folk got up this early."

"I wouldn't exactly call myself a city person. Charleston isn't like New York or Los Angeles. Have you ever been?"

"No, but I'd like to see it someday."

"I know just the place to take you." Abby's exhilaration lit her face and instantly Clay envisioned himself walking through the historic city with Abby by his side.

He cleared his throat. "I can, uh, spend a few hours with you this morning before I have to get to work. I have a full load between your case and a couple others. A good portion of my day will be online and back at the courthouse. I swear I should just move my office in there."

"I thought you said you don't have one." Abby closed her car door and walked in his direction. Her barely there makeup and still-damp hair, which fell past her shoulders in waves, accentuated her natural beauty.

"I don't." Clay strained to focus on the conversation. "I work out of my house, which is a sore subject right now. I've thought about renting some space in town, especially after one of my clients chastised me for meeting her in a luncheonette."

Abby jutted her chin upward. "I didn't chastise you. I just questioned it. It seemed a little odd."

Clay chuckled. "Well, don't just stand there." He motioned for Abby to follow him. "Let's get you on a horse."

"I didn't realize you had so many animals." She stopped to peer into one of the pigpens. "You don't kill them, do you?"

Her big forget-me-not blue eyes gazed up at him. "Abby, where do you think bacon comes from?"

"I know, but—"

"Relax," Clay reassured. "Here's the deal, and I'm only telling you this to prove what a stooge I am. Money's tight in these parts. Farming and ranching isn't what it used to be, and when my clients can't pay me in cash I end up with one of their animals in payment. The horse you'll be riding happens to be one of those payments. So no, I don't kill them. I house them, feed them, and watch my bank account dwindle because of them."

"I think I found another reason to like you." Abby walked into the barn.

"Thanks, I think." The extra beat his heart took at her comment unnerved Clay. He didn't want a relationship with Abby. Correction. He didn't need a relationship with Abby. But damned if his body didn't betray him at the thought.

Clay took a moment to steady himself before entering the barn. He clipped lead ropes to each horse's halter. "This is Olivia." Clay led the Welsh pony out alongside Dream Catcher.

"They look like twins." Abby ran her hand over Olivia's platinum mane and across her slate-gray back. The horse turned, giving Abby the once-over. "She's not as small as I thought she would be."

"She's almost thirteen hands, which in layman's terms would be a little over four feet to her withers."

"Withers?" Abby asked.

"The highest part of the horse's back, at the base of the neck." Clay ran his hand over the horse's shoulder before heading back into the barn for Olivia's saddle and bridle.

"Why do they measure in hands?" Abby asked when he returned.

"A hand is four inches." Clay placed a small pad and blanket on the pony's back before adding the saddle. "Measuring in *hands* dates back to ancient Egyptian times where a hand was the equivalent of the width of a male adult hand. It's a custom that's survived thousands of years."

"How tall is your horse?"

"Dream Catcher is a Morgan and he is 15.2 hands high. He's actually at the top of the height range for his breed." After tightening the saddle cinch straps, Clay removed Olivia's halter and slipped a bitless bridle over the pony's head. "Ready to hop on?"

"Approach from the left side, correct?" Abby asked.

"I take it Gracie taught you some basic horsemanship yesterday when you were at Dance of Hope." Clay smiled. "Sorry I couldn't stay, and while I'm apologizing, I'm sorry for running out on you the other night. Believe me when I tell you, it's nothing you've done wrong. You're perfect."

Abby's eyes widened. "Well, thank you."

"That's not what I meant." Yeah, *that* was the perfect response.

"Alrighty then." Abby moved closer to Olivia. "Moving on."

"I'm not saying you're not perfect." Clay fumbled for the right words. "Oh, forget it. I'm sorry I put you on the spot and kissed you in front of everyone."

"I'm not." Abby faced Clay. Less than a foot separated them. "I rather enjoyed it while it lasted."

Abby's matter-of-factness caught Clay off guard. Placing his hands on her shoulders, he turned her around to face Olivia. For the briefest of moments he wanted to pull her close and wrap his arms around her. "Place your foot in the stirrup, get a good hop going and swing your leg over."

With the agility of a dancer, Abby hopped once and slid into the saddle like a seasoned pro.

"I love their coloring." She leaned forward and hugged Olivia's neck.

"It's called silver dapple and only a few breeds have it."

"Their manes and tails are as blond as I am." Abby shifted slightly in her saddle and patted the pony. "I think she looks like me, don't you?"

"You don't have her dark roots, at least not that I can tell, anyway," Clay teased. "If you look closely at her mane, you'll notice her roots are quite a bit darker. Her eyelashes are blond and both Olivia's and Dream Catcher's legs fade from gray to almost white. Their hooves are what is known as *striped,* meaning they're white with darker stripes running vertically in them."

"Aren't you riding with me?" Abby looked at Dream Catcher still loosely tied to a hitching post. "He doesn't have a saddle."

Clay shook his head. "I'm going to turn Dream Catcher out in the pasture before I walk you around on Olivia. I want you to get the nitty-gritties down before we head out on a trail."

Teaching Abby how to ride a horse was the last thing he wanted to do. Well, that wasn't entirely true. If he were honest, he'd admit he had looked forward to the lesson. He had actually wondered if Abby would show.

Abby remained focused on Clay's instruction as he led her around. Accepting the pony in return for payment had been an unexpected burden, but this morning, he was grateful that his client hadn't had the cash to pay him.

For someone who'd never ridden, Abby exuded more confidence than he had expected, though her death grip on the saddle horn told a different story. She was slightly afraid, and that was okay. She may not know how to hold the reins or where to place her feet, but she knew how to sit up straight in the saddle. Probably due to Gracie's teaching yesterday.

"Be gentle with me." Abby's smile made Clay want to grasp the back of her head and pull her close for a kiss. She definitely knew how to test his resolve.

"I wouldn't have it any other way." *What the heck was that?* He shouldn't flirt with her, yet that's exactly what he was doing.

"Have you ever taught someone how to ride before?" Abby asked.

"A few people." Clay adjusted the length of her stirrups, trying to avoid touching her shapely calf at the same time. "Some bigger, some smaller than you. I know sneakers are comfortable, but if you're going to ride a horse, you really need a boot with a small heel. They don't have to be cowboy boots, they can be lace-up ropers, but you need something that will prevent your feet from sliding through the stirrups. And that doesn't mean a four-inch heel."

"Ha, ha. There's a place across from the Bark Park."

"Cowpokes." Clay nodded.

"Why don't we go there after our lesson?" The casualness of Abby's question made him feel like they were an old married couple.

"I'm not going shoe shopping with you so I can hold your purse," Clay said. "Plus, if you ever expect me to solve your case, I have to actually work."

"Fine, I'll ask Bridgett. I need to stop in and see her mom anyway. Quirky woman, but then again, aren't we all?"

"Some more than others," Clay jested.

Abby swatted him from atop Olivia. Now would have been the perfect time to kiss her. They were alone, with no audience to heckle or cheer them on. But a kiss was out of the question. Wasn't it?

"I can't believe I'm learning how to ride on the kids' pony."

And the moment was gone. *Dammit.*

"Welsh ponies are preferred by many adults. Someone my size can't ride one, but there's no reason why you can't. They're one of the more intelligent breeds and extremely surefooted, which makes them the perfect beginner horse."

"So what's the first part of my lesson?"

Clay moved closer to Abby, guiding her hands over the reins, showing her how to hold them loosely. The moment his skin made contact with hers, his pulse quickened and beads of sweat formed on the back of his neck.

"Trust the horse over yourself. Your instinct will be to grip the reins tightly. That'll only make for a very tense horse. If you remain relaxed, the horse will, too." Advice he needed to follow himself.

"What do you say, Olivia?" Abby patted the horse's neck. "You ready to show Clay what we're made of?"

Clay laughed. Any nervousness she may have felt earlier was gone. In a matter of minutes, she'd taken to the animal, and he was glad one of them was calm because his nerves were more on edge than before an ATF raid.

"THANK YOU FOR the lesson." Abby walked alongside Clay as they exited the barn after putting up the horse's tack. "I appreciate you taking the time out of your day. Before I get out of your hair, may I use your bathroom? My bladder's been jostled more than I can handle."

"I, uh, sure," Clay said. "But please excuse the mess. I'm still trying to decide what to do with the downstairs, so there are quite a few boxes around."

She followed him into the house. *A few boxes* was the understatement of the year. While the kitchen was bare except for Clay's files spread across the counter and the table, the dark dining room contained stacks of boxes, haphazardly scattered around the room. The living room was behind there somewhere, but she couldn't see it. The blinds were closed, and with the exception of the kitchen light, barely any light filtered into the rooms.

"The water closet's right here." Clay squeezed past Abby and opened a narrow door containing a toilet. "You'll have to use the kitchen sink to wash up. The previous owner converted the pantry into a bathroom of sorts."

"Thanks." Abby closed the door behind her. It was small but clean and that's all that mattered.

When she exited, she spotted Clay waiting for her near the stove. She peeked into the dining room again as she headed for the sink.

"I hate unpacking," Abby said as she washed her hands. "When I moved to Charleston, it took me months to find a place for everything. When did you move in?"

When he didn't answer, Abby looked up to see Clay staring at the Stetson in his hands. "Are you okay?"

"This is embarrassing." He took a deep breath and met her eyes. "I bought this place when I moved back to town three years ago."

"Oh." Abby dried her hands on a dish towel hanging from a drawer handle. The house looked as if he had moved in yesterday. "Slow unpacker, huh?"

"I don't want you to get the wrong idea." Clay ran his hand through his hair. "I'm not one of those hoarders you see on television."

"I'm not saying you are." She wanted to ask questions, but she didn't want to push him away. The darkness, the boxes, combined with the things she'd heard and the way he ran off on her, told Abby there was more to Clay's story than just a broken heart. "I'm here if you want to talk."

He nodded, not offering any more details.

"Again, I appreciate the lesson this morning." She closed the short distance between them and gave him a quick hug goodbye. His arms encircled her, holding her close. This was the hug she had wanted the day they had met, only today Clay was the one who needed comforting.

"Thank you, Abby," Clay whispered against her hair.

"Anytime." She withdrew slightly and looked up at him. "I feel more and more that Walter knew I would come here when he wrote me that note. Especially after spending the afternoon at Dance of Hope. What I can't figure out is if he knew I'd hire someone to help me."

"I don't think I was part of his plans." Clay eased his hold on her. "I do think there is some validity to your coming here. I can't say for certain yet, but I believe a few people know something." Clay's hands slid from around her back and up to her shoulders. "I shouldn't be telling you this, but I'm just going to lay it out. I'm attracted to you. I'm feeling things again I didn't know were possible and it confuses the hell out of me. I broke the golden P.I. rule when I met you—an ethical investigator never gets personally involved with a client. You're paying me to do a job and there I was, kissing you on stage at Slater's Mill, and now I'm hugging you in my kitchen. I know it's wrong, but I don't know how to stop."

"Wh—what are you saying?" Did he want to be with her or was he walking away? Abby knew they didn't have long-term potential, especially when she was scheduled to leave in a little over a week. That didn't mean she wasn't hopeful at the possibility of some sort of romance.

Clay rubbed his jaw. "I excused it at first. I told myself I was infatuated with a woman who'd be in town just for a few days. Then yesterday when Kay offered you a job, my heart went from *it's not possible* to *dang, she's obtainable* in a matter of minutes. My brain's telling me to focus on my job and keep my distance, when all I want to do is help you find the answers you're looking for. Please, Abby, respect me enough to know I'll do the best I can, but understand it may not be enough."

"I believe you." She didn't know why she placed all

her faith in a virtual stranger, and it didn't matter. The fact that Clay thought about stepping over the line for her told Abby all she needed to know. "But as far as moving to Ramblewood, Clay, I don't think I can."

Clay gathered her into his arms, his hands locking against her spine. Dipping his mouth to hers, his lips touched hers. She softened against him, lifting her hands to his face, feeling the rough stubble of his morning beard in her palms. Her lips parted, her tongue leisurely exploring his. She stood on her toes, and Clay lifted her. Her legs instinctively wrapped around his waist, allowing her to feel the full length of his arousal.

With more urgency, Clay's mouth hungrily claimed hers. Abby's breath quickened, her breasts aching against his chest. Clay pulled back and stared into her eyes, his breath fanning her cheek.

"If I don't let you leave now, you never will." Clay eased Abby onto her feet. "I want you, but not when I have to leave in a few minutes. When I make love to you, it will be slow and deliberate…and I promise we'll both need the next day to recover."

"You're very sure of yourself." Abby fought to steady her shallow breaths.

"I'm sure of only one thing, Abby. Whatever this is between you and me, it's worth exploring. I hope you'll decide to stay in Ramblewood because I'd hate to miss out on doing this for the rest of my life."

Abby chewed her bottom lip. Yeah, that love thing she hadn't experienced, she was pretty sure this was how it started.

Chapter Six

After Abby left, Clay cooled off with a long cold shower. Halfway through, he heard singing, then realized it was his own voice. Laughing, he quickly dressed and made himself a cup of coffee to get his head back in the game.

He ran a few background checks for the dating agency, then flipped through Abby's file once again. One thing was strange about her birth certificate. In place of a hospital was an address, which wasn't uncommon if a baby was born at home. To someone unfamiliar with birth certificates, they'd probably assume it was the hospital's. Since Abby hadn't mentioned it, Clay wondered if she even knew where she was physically born. But, it was this particular address that drew him in.

"That's out near Miranda and Jesse Langtry's place."

Typing the address into his laptop, Clay fell backward in the chair when the results appeared on the screen.

"Abby was born on Double Trouble." Miranda had bought the ranch when she won the Maryland state lottery a few years ago. The former owners, Ed and Fran Carter had died in a car accident, and Fran's sister had sold the entire estate to the highest bidder. Jesse Langtry, one of Kay's sons, had been a horse trainer on Double Trouble since high school. He had planned to buy the ranch once the Carters retired. When Miranda outbid him, he had been devastated. Eventually, Miranda and Jesse had fallen for each other and married.

Hmm. Abby had already been born by the time Jesse started working at Double Trouble. Mable Promise on the other hand, Miranda's surrogate mother of sorts, had resided on Double Trouble way back when her husband had managed the place. She still lived there.

Clay grabbed his phone off the counter and ran out the back door. A birth was a big event for a small town, yet he had never heard it mentioned. A heavy feeling formed in the pit of his stomach. Something definitely wasn't right.

He pulled into the Double Trouble Ranch a short time later and spotted Beau Bradley's pickup parked near Mable's small white cottage, which was nestled behind the main house.

Rumor had it the widow and widower had a romance brewing. He knew them both well enough to presume he wasn't interrupting an afternoon delight. His instincts told him their visit concerned Abby.

Mable met Clay at the screen door. "If you come in here you keep your voice down," she hissed. "I just got those young'uns down for a nap, and Lord help anyone who wakes them. They've been fussin' all morning and Miranda is just about ready to come off her spool."

"Yes, ma'am." Clay removed his hat and stepped into the living room. Miranda and Jesse's twins, Jackson and Slade, were a little over a year old, and true to Langtry form, rabble-rousers from day one.

Beau appeared in the kitchen doorway and acknowledged Clay with a slight head nod. "What brings you around?"

"I think you know, but I'll ask anyway." Clay directed his attention back to Mable, who hadn't stopped wringing her hands since his arrival. "Abby Winchester—Beau knows who she is—as I'm sure you've heard, hired me to find her sister. Turns out Abby was born here, on Double Trouble almost twenty-eight years ago. Do you remember her parents?"

Mable's cinnamon-colored cheeks pinkened. "I was away visiting my brother that week. I heard about it when I returned. Her parents were long gone by then. I don't know anything else."

"Nothing at all?" Mable was one of the most kind-hearted and honest people he knew, but her words seemed rehearsed and unnatural. He did find it interesting that Mable said the Davidsons had left town after the baby was born, because that part was true. During his preliminary research, Clay had noted Abby's parents moved two days later. "Mable, think back. Did you ever hear the Carters or anyone discuss Abby's family? Her father's name was Walter Davidson and he was stationed at Randolph Air Force Base. Does that mean anything to you?"

Mable shook her head and looked to Beau. "Did you know Walter Davidson or—" She turned back to Clay. "What is her mother's name?"

"Maeve." Clay narrowed his eyes at Beau. "They rented an apartment in town. Someone must have known them, and Beau, I love you like a member of my own family, but I feel there's something you're purposely not telling me."

"What makes you say that?" The older man shifted slightly against the doorjamb.

"You have this particular *tell* when you're bluffing. I saw it the other night at Slater's, right before you ran out on our conversation."

Beau stiffened. "What tell?" Clay noticed his old friend didn't bother to deny ducking out on him.

"If I told you, I wouldn't be able to beat you at cards anymore." He had the man's attention now. "I'm good at my job. Whatever you're hiding, I'll find out anyway. Why not save us both the aggravation?"

A muffled cry came from down the hallway.

"That does it." Mable swatted them both toward the door. "Out you go. I told you not to wake those babies, now get out of here."

Mable brusquely shoved Beau and Clay through the doorway. When Clay turned back, the screen slammed in his face.

"That didn't go as planned." Clay sized up his old friend. "Beau, I respect you and I'm only going to ask you once, please don't get in the middle of my investigation."

"The way I see it, you put me in the middle by confronting me."

"What are you so defensive about? What does Abby have to do with—" Clay smiled when the realization struck him. Beau had worked for the Carters back then. "You were here the night she was born, weren't you?"

"You don't know what you're talking about." Beau spat. "Leave this alone."

Before Clay could ask the man another question, Beau stormed off the porch and hurried to his truck. Within seconds, Clay was staring into a cloud of dust.

"What got his dander up today?" Jesse called from the corral nearest the cottage. "He's been in and out of here quite a bit lately."

Clay strode to the fence and watched Jesse lengthen the lunge rope as the horse he trained circled the pen. Jesse was the one Langtry brother who didn't reside on Bridle Dance land.

"Have you gotten around to sorting through those file boxes you found in the attic?" Clay asked.

Jesse slowed the horse to a walk and tilted his hat off his face.

"Are you kidding me? The boys will be grown and away at college before we get around to tackling that mess. Why?"

"Mind if I poke around up there? I'm working a case, and it turns out the woman was born here, on your ranch. I'm hoping I might come across something…a diary, receipts or some clue leading me in the right direction."

"Are you talking about Abby?" Jesse shortened the lunge rope and walked the horse toward the fence.

"Mable and Beau both worked here when Abby was born, yet neither of them admit to being around that day. They say they don't remember her parents, and I believe they're hiding the truth for whatever reason."

"Have at it." Jesse nodded toward the house. "Miranda's not home—she needed a baby break, so go on in. Be careful up there. I haven't checked the floor out yet. If it's anything like the downstairs, there might be a few weak boards. Have you talked to my mom? She knows everyone."

"Abby has, but the names didn't ring a bell. She did find out that Alfred Anderson has boxes of photos from every Ramblewood function known to man. They're going to go through them and see if Abby can find one of her parents."

"Good luck." Jesse pulled his hat down low. "I'm going to take Majesty out with the herd and see how we do today. He's been a slow learner. I have my phone on me in case you fall through the attic floor."

Clay laughed. "Gee, thanks."

He glanced toward Mable's cottage before he headed

toward the farm house. The woman boldly stood in the doorway watching him. Why the secrecy surrounding Abby's birth?

"Hɪᴛ ᴍᴇ." Aʙʙʏ dropped onto one of the stools at the counter of The Magpie. "And a slice of pie. You choose the kind."

"I think there a few slices of lemon meringue left," Bridgett said. "It's been so busy here this morning I haven't had a chance to get into the kitchen. I'd much rather be back there baking than up front any day."

"Are you really happy here?" Abby couldn't understand why someone with the desire to bake stayed in a waitressing job. "Have you thought about cooking school?"

"I can't afford it." Bridgett straightened her apron. "Not on this salary. I'm more the self-taught type anyway. College and trade school weren't exactly on my radar."

"Fair enough." Abby hated to see people settle, though, and a part of her wondered if that's what she was doing by staying in Charleston. After Clay's mind-numbing kiss earlier, followed by his declaration, she had decided she needed to get to work on that pros-and-cons list.

"Be right back." Bridgett twirled and glided toward the kitchen. No dance class in the world would give Abby the gracefulness Bridgett possessed.

A minute later, she set a slice of pie on the counter. "My God," Abby said. "There must be five inches of meringue on this thing."

"I swear every time Maggie makes it, she piles it higher."

"Who's the new waitress?" Abby looked in the direction of a woman bussing a table near the front window.

"That's Lark Meadow. Like the name?" Bridgett

cocked her head. "She rolled in to town yesterday on the bus. Walked in here with a guitar strapped to her back and Maggie hired her on the spot."

"Where's she from?" Abby asked, happy she wasn't the only newcomer in town.

"New Mexico." Bridgett poured Abby a cup of coffee. "Said she was on her way back there after auditioning in Nashville. Claims she sold everything she owned before leaving and doesn't have a home to go to anymore. Maggie helped her rent a small studio apartment above the florist shop across the street. I suspect Maggie fronted the deposit and Lark will be paying it off for a long time to come."

"Is she working out okay?" Abby noted the hard edge to Lark's appearance. It wasn't just the choppy layered hair and dark eye makeup, Lark's face was gaunt, as if she hadn't slept in days. Whatever her story was, it appeared to be a rough one.

"Seems to be. Definitely has waitressing experience. All the busybodies in town had to check her out, which is why we're swamped today." Bridgett shook her head. "I get the feeling Lark's running from something or someone, but it's not my place to ask. Besides, I'm hoping with her out front, I can get in more baking time."

"How's your mom feeling? Usually the first day after physical therapy is the toughest."

"Sore, but she didn't have her usual stiffness this morning."

"Just so you know, her leg did heal beautifully after the fall. But she favored it so much she threw her whole body out of alignment." Abby lowered her voice so their conversation wouldn't be overheard. "Don't say anything to your mom yet, but I plan on talking to Gracie at Dance of Hope to see if she thinks your mom could benefit from some hippotherapy."

Bridgett grinned. "Thank you for doing this. Mom appreciates it even though she may have a strange way of showing her gratitude. She'd love to get on one of those horses." Bridgett leaned close. "Speaking of love and horses...I heard you had a riding lesson with the P.I. this morning."

"How did you hear that?" The only person who knew she was visiting Clay was Mazie, and she didn't think the woman ran to the luncheonette to spread the news.

"Seems your little Mini Cooper is quite the attraction in truck country. A few people mentioned they saw you heading in Clay's direction earlier."

"I could've been going anywhere. That's not to say that I didn't see Clay, because I did, but still."

"Honey, this is a small town." Bridgett flicked her ponytail. "You have to get used to the gossip, especially if you take Kay up on her job offer. Why didn't you tell me that when you came over last night to see my mom?"

Just how fast does news travel around here?

"Because last night was about your mom and I wanted to focus on her evaluation." She shrugged. "Besides, I haven't made a decision about Dance of Hope yet. It's an appealing proposition, but I don't think it's doable. In addition to the financial considerations, I can't leave my patients like that. Many of them are long-term, and even though I'm away for two weeks on vacation, they know I'll return. My brother, my friends and my life are in Charleston."

"Give me a second to take care of these customers." Bridgett gestured at an incoming couple. "When I get back, you'd better be ready to dish, girl."

Abby still reeled from her passionate encounter with

Clay in his kitchen. If he hadn't stopped, she didn't think she would've found the strength. She was still curious about the boxes and the darkened rooms. When she had returned to the Bed & Biscuit, Abby had searched the internet for Clay's name again, hoping to discover an explanation. But outside of Clay's high school sports days, nothing appeared online. Of course, she knew none of his work with the ATF would be available for the whole world to see.

"Okay, I'm back. Start talking." Bridgett rested her arms on the counter, eyes sparkling.

"I showed up at his house uninvited this morning. Well, we'd talked about it yesterday at Bridle Dance, but we hadn't settled on when. Even though Clay was surprised to see me, he made the time to give me a lesson. It was fun...he's a good teacher."

"Uh-huh."

"Uh-huh, what?"

"Where's the rest of the story?" Bridgett smirked. "And don't tell me there isn't one because I can tell you kissed him again."

"How could you possibly know that?" Abby asked. "We were in his kitchen. No one else was there."

"Honestly, I didn't know until you just told me." Bridgett folded her arms in satisfaction.

"I can't believe you tricked me and I fell for it." Abby shook her head. "Okay, yes, I kissed him. It was hot and wonderful and he didn't run away this time." She held up her hands. "And before you say it, yes, I still have my life jacket on."

"I think we can upgrade you to water wings now," Bridgett quipped. "So what happened next?"

"Nothing. He had work to do and I had to take a cold

shower. This isn't fair. You know far more about me than I do you. Who are you involved with?"

"No one and I won't be until I find Mr. Right. When I was in high school I pretty much dated…well…everyone. One day I realized I was dating guys just to date them. I was one of those girls who had to have a boyfriend and I let it define me. These days, I'm more selective. Who knows when or if Mr. Right will walk through that door, but I'll be ready for him."

"How will you know it's the right guy?"

Bridgett shrugged. "It's not like I've ever been in a serious, long-term relationship. I think I'll feel it in my heart. Isn't that what love is? That deep down, undeniable sense of belonging and peace with someone?"

Abby laughed. "You're asking the wrong person. I'm in the same boat as you are. I've never been in love myself."

Abby wasn't sure if Clay was *the one,* if Dance of Hope was the right job or if Ramblewood was the right town in the search for her sister. The only thing she had to go on was that everything was coming together at the same time. The pieces fit. Maybe Ramblewood wasn't where she was supposed to start her search, and maybe Walter had been delusional when he'd written his note. It didn't seem to matter. She was exploring her options. Whether she took advantage of them or not, she liked having them for once.

Abby stood and placed money on the counter for the pie and coffee. "I'm going to stop across the street and see how your mom's doing. When you get off work, would you like to go shopping with me? Clay said I need a more riding-appropriate shoe."

"Sure, I have another half hour. I'll meet you at the

salon. My mom called in a late lunch order and I told her I would drop it off."

"Sounds like a plan."

Outside, Abby walked to the corner. She didn't cross the street immediately. From where she stood, the town unfolded in all directions. Closing her eyes, she raised her face to the sky and inhaled. The air was different here than it was at home. Not to say one was better than the other. Simply different. Charleston had a heavier, saltier smell. Ramblewood had a crisp, laundry-on-the-line scent, with a hint of sweetness to it.

In Ramblewood, there were no sounds of horses' hooves on cobblestone streets. She was accustomed to seeing horses every day in Charleston, thanks to the many carriage tours of the historic district. It was almost expected. But here in the heart of Hill Country, where horses and cowboys were the norm, she couldn't envision a horse riding down Main Street. It would seem out of character. Almost ironic.

Smiling, Abby crossed the street to the Curl Up & Dye. The salon bustled with customers while Kylie happily bopped behind the counter to a Blake Shelton song. Every manicure station was in use, and there was Ruby, in the thick of it, laughing heartily while airbrushing someone's nails.

"Here she is." Ruby waved Abby over. "Were your ears burning? I was talking about you less than a minute ago." She tapped the customer's hand. "Isn't she beautiful? She's dating our Mr. Tanner."

"Whoa." Abby held up her hands. "I don't know if I'd say dating."

"We also heard you might be moving to Ramblewood," said the woman whose nails Ruby was intricately painting. "I'm Charlotte Hargrove, by the way. Very nice to meet you."

"Same here." Abby's heart began pounding like a trapped rabbit's. "I haven't made any decisions yet. My main focus is finding my sister."

"Yes, I heard about that. How exciting to have a long-lost relative. I wish I could lose some of mine. You can have them if you want." Charlotte's response was met with laughter from the other women in the salon, cluing Abby in on just how many people were hanging on her every word.

By the time Bridgett appeared with Ruby's lunch order, Abby was exhausted from answering questions about herself.

"Hello, everyone...Mother." Bridgett leaned over and gave Ruby a quick kiss on the cheek. "Abby and I are going shopping. I'll see you back at the house for dinner."

Ruby looked up from where she sat and stared at Bridgett and then Abby. "You two have fun," she said, her voice fragile, almost shaking.

As Abby and Bridgett walked out of the salon, Abby whispered, "Is your mom okay? She looked upset."

"She's been a little off lately." Bridgett peered through the salon window, studying her mother. "I thought it was her leg at first, but now I'm not so sure." She sighed. "I wish she'd meet someone. My mom's the life of the party, but the minute everyone goes home, she retreats inside herself. I think she has a thing for the man who owns the movie theater, but she'll never admit to it. It's so obvious... how many times a week can you possibly go to the movies by yourself?"

Abby hoped it was a romance that kept Ruby in the confines of the dark theater and not her injury. She'd seen too many of her patients battle depression when they were no longer able to do what they once could. The thought made Abby anxious to get back to Charleston. Her job was more than a paycheck. It had become her world and each patient an extension of herself. Ramblewood may be calling to her, but home was Charleston, and she didn't know how she'd be able to leave it.

CLAY HAD SPENT the entire afternoon and a good portion of the evening poring through the files in the attic of the Double Trouble ranch. Miranda had insisted he join them for dinner and he had. After, he and Jesse searched more boxes, but he still came up empty. However, they had discovered quite a few historical papers about the house and land that Miranda planned to frame.

When he'd checked in with Abby on his way home, she had excitedly told him about her shopping trip followed by dinner with Bridgett and Ruby. She'd asked if they'd have another lesson in the morning, and as much as he would've loved to have said yes, he'd already fallen behind on too many of his cases. He needed to remain focused on work. If he got within ten feet of Abby, he'd be all over her. And the next time he'd like to be able to continue…

After working through the night in an attempt to catch up, Clay managed to drag himself to The Magpie the following morning for a bite to eat and a cup of coffee. Somewhere around midnight, he'd scooped the last bit of ground coffee from the metal can on the counter. Clay had no food in the house. The last time he had stepped inside a grocery store was a sour gallon of milk ago. Outside of beer and some eggs from the chickens, he was pretty much out of everything.

"Breakfast for one this morning or is Abby on her

way?" Bridgett turned over his cup and filled it with coffee.

"Just me. I have some work to finish before I head to the courthouse later." He hadn't considered calling Abby and asking her to meet him for breakfast. It was barely seven. Would she be up? "I heard you two had a great time yesterday."

"We did. Abby and I have more in common than I thought we would. I really like her and I especially like her with you. Just don't break her heart," Bridgett warned. "What can I get you today?"

"The breakfast special," Clay said, laughing at Bridgett's unexpected comment. "And a carafe of coffee."

"An all-nighter?" Bridgett smiled. "I guess that's the beauty of working from home. Your order will be out in a few."

She clipped his order to the stainless-steel ticket wheel and told the cook, Bert, to make it a priority. Clay appreciated the gesture, and he appreciated her friendship with Abby. In the same breath, the fact that Bridgett liked him with Abby scared Clay. Abby deserved someone to give a hundred percent of themselves to her. He didn't know if he could…at least, not yet.

His body told him he was ready to move on, but his heart lagged behind. The guilt of kissing Abby had lessened, but it still existed. He wanted to be happy again, but wanting and deserving were two different entities. The responsibility he carried for Ana Rosa's and Paulo's deaths haunted him every day. He needed to move on from the pain. Whenever Abby was around, he saw a glimmer of what might be, along with the betrayal of his love for Ana Rosa. And even though he was willing to try the long-distance thing, it was probably wise to slow things until she made a decision.

"Don't you have a birthday coming up?" Clay overheard a customer ask Bridgett.

"October thirteenth." Bridgett groaned. Clay jotted down a note to remind himself to wish her a happy birthday. "I still have a month to go."

"I could have sworn it was this month. I pride myself on my memory, you know. Twenty-eight this year, right?" the woman prodded further.

"Don't remind me," Bridgett sighed. "Can't we say twenty-one for the seventh time?"

Bemused by Bridgett's fear of aging, Clay laughed to himself for a moment, then the realization of what he had heard set in. He quickly flipped through his note pad. Abby's birthdate struck him square in the jaw. Clay looked across the luncheonette at Bridgett. He was searching for Abby's sister—he may have just found her twin.

Chapter Seven

Abby grinned when she came downstairs with Duffy for their morning Bark Park visit and found Janie's husband, Alfred, standing in the front parlor with two file boxes next to him.

"You didn't have to bring these here. I would've gone to your house." The number of black-and-white photos Alfred spread across the coffee table amazed Abby. "Janie was right when she said you photographed everyone in town."

"Coming here gave me an excuse to drive Janie crazy while she works." The older man winked at Abby before waving to his wife who stood in the foyer. "I narrowed these down to a few years before and after you were born. I can always expand the search more in one direction or the other, but this gives us a good place to start."

Abby flipped through the white-edged photos, admiring the sharp detail Alfred had captured in each of his subjects. It contrasted with the soft blur of the background.

"These are really good," she said. "Did you develop them yourself?"

"Yep." Alfred sat a little straighter and nodded. "After I retired, it gave me something to do. Janie says I spend too much time in my darkroom."

"Now it's all he does." Janie took a seat next to her husband on the double-ended burgundy jacquard Victorian sofa. "Your search gave him reason to organize some of this stuff."

"Why didn't you ever become a professional photographer?" Abby thumbed through another mound. "You're really good."

"Because then it would be work and I wouldn't enjoy it as much," Alfred said. "This way, I'm not on anyone's schedule except my own."

Janie cleared her throat. "And mine."

"Yes, dear." Alfred patted his wife's knee. "Yours, too."

The love radiating between the couple warmed Abby. If she didn't already know they were married, she wouldn't have guessed the much older Alfred was Janie's husband. Fifteen years or more separated them, but their adoration for each other outshone the difference in their ages. She dreamed of that kind of love—where every day retained some newlywed bliss.

"Oh, my gosh!" Abby's hand flew to her chest. "This is Walter."

Judging by the year on the back of the photograph, Abby was three when it had been taken. Long after her parents had divorced and left Ramblewood.

"I took that during the annual Harvest Festival, which is only a few weeks away," Alfred said.

"What are the chances you and your father came to Ramblewood the same time of year, twenty-five years apart from each other?"

"It's not by chance." A tear trailed down her cheek. "He would have been here for my birthday. Just as he sent me here now. I'm in the right place. My sister's here."

Janie squeezed Abby's hand. "Let me see the picture, dear."

Duffy jumped onto Abby's lap, as he always did when he sensed she was upset. "It's okay." She held him close to her chest. "Mommy's all right. She's just one step closer to the truth."

The excitement over her quest stilled, suddenly turning to apprehension. Her friend Angela's words echoed in her head. *Are you sure this is a good idea?* Cold tingles crept up Abby's spine. No matter the outcome of her search, her life would never be the same after this trip.

A part of her wanted to run—to leave and forget she knew anything about a long-lost sister. But, no. She knew too much now. There was no turning back.

"That's Darren Fox with your father," Janie said, snapping Abby to attention.

"Who?"

"The mayor. Well, the mayor now. He wasn't back then," Alfred said. "Based on the way they're facing each other, I'd say they're having a conversation."

Abby examined the photograph again. It was hard to tell exactly what was going on in the picture, but if the mayor knew her father she had a new place to start looking for answers.

"Do you mind if I borrow this?" Abby asked Alfred. "I'd like to take it with me when I talk to the mayor."

"Of course you can," he said. "You'll have to wait to see Darren, though. He left on a fishing trip a few days ago. Not sure when he'll be back."

"Talk about bad timing," Abby said. "I arrive in town looking for my sister and the only tie to my biological father takes off?"

"I'm sure it's a coincidence," Janie said, but Abby didn't miss the look that passed between the woman and her husband. They felt it, too. Something was definitely amiss.

CLAY FOUGHT TO WRAP his head around the likelihood that Abby and Bridgett were sisters. He needed to be absolutely certain before he even hinted at the possibility to Abby.

Question after question churned in his head. He vaguely remembered when Bridgett had been born. He'd been only five years old. And Ruby. She'd been a wild one in her day, and she still had her moments…but secret twins? That would mean Abby's mother, Maeve, wasn't her biological mother.

"This will devastate Abby." It was the part of the job Clay hated the most. Telling people the things they paid him to uncover wasn't always pleasant, especially when it meant telling them the life they knew was a lie. And Abby's life wasn't the only one about to be upended. Bridgett, Ruby, Abby's parents…this revelation would hurt all of them.

He stopped his truck at Ramblewood's one and only traffic light on the corner of Main and Shelby. Abby was inside the Bed & Biscuit, yards away from the Curl Up & Dye Salon. Was it possible Abby's biological mother was only a few yards away and she didn't know of her existence?

Clay's phone rang. Abby. She couldn't have fit the pieces together. Then again, maybe she had. His phone trilled a third time. Once more and it would go to voice mail. Knowing she might be watching him from one of the windows at the Bed & Biscuit, he answered the phone.

"Hello." Clay looked toward the inn and saw Abby waving to him from the front porch.

"Clay, can you see me?" Abby asked breathlessly. "That's you at the corner, isn't it?"

"Yes." He honked his horn.

"Turn right, will you?" She paused. Did she sense his

hesitation? "Alfred has a photo of Walter and the mayor that I want to show you."

Darren Fox? "The current mayor or one from years ago?"

"I'll tell you when you get here." Exasperation was evident in her voice.

Without another word, she hung up. Clay hated facing Abby before he had any more information. Taking a deep breath, his ATF training clicked into high gear. Hiding the truth was second nature to him. He had worked undercover long enough to be able to convincingly lie to anyone, including Ana Rosa, the woman he'd loved. Why should today be any different?

Because it was Abby.

Clay wasn't sure he'd be able to pull off lying to… *to what?* The new woman he loved? No way. It was too soon. They barely knew each other. And after Abby heard the truth about her family, or who she thought was her family, she might never want another thing to do with him. He'd forever be known as the man who destroyed her life.

He parked in front of the Bed & Biscuit, dispensing with the adjacent lot. Willing himself from the truck, he trudged up the porch stairs, gathering every ounce of composure he could muster.

The door swung wide and Abby grabbed him by the hand, leading him to the sitting room. Alfred and Janie Anderson searched through stacks of old photographs, while Mazie cleared more room on the end tables for them to spread out.

"Look." Abby thrust a photo into his hand. "That's Walter. It's the only one we've found so far, but that's him. That's my biological father."

Clay turned the photo over, noting the date. Was it

possible Walter had been visiting Bridgett? If the man was in town years after Abby was born, then maybe he'd had a relationship with Ruby all along. Abby did say her mother had quickly dismissed the sister story and Abby herself had wondered if Walter had had an affair.

"Well?" Abby stared up at him. "Don't you have anything to say?"

"Give me a minute," Clay pleaded. "I'm running through a few scenarios in my head." It wasn't an outright lie.

Darren Fox was definitely the other man in the picture. From the angle it was taken, it was hard to tell if they were simply standing near each other during the Harvest Festival parade or if they were in the middle of a conversation. Clay remembered hearing that Darren was in the Air Force back in the day, so it was possible the two men knew each other.

"No luck finding any others, huh?" Clay asked.

Abby sat silently in one of the arm chairs, her back and shoulders rigid. She began flipping through another stack.

"Not yet," Mazie answered, instead. "I'm looking to see if I can find one of Darren."

Clay feared Abby was about to stumble across a shot of Walter and Ruby together. None of this made sense. If Walter had had an affair with Ruby, why were the girls separated at birth? What would possess Ruby to do such a thing…unless one baby was stolen. Clay was grasping for answers, not wanting to face the fact the babies might have been purposely separated.

"Abby." Clay crouched beside her chair. "I know this is difficult and you want immediate answers. You've made great progress and I'm going to talk to Darren to see if he remembers—"

"You can't," Abby interrupted. "Darren took off on a fishing trip somewhere." Immediately Clay wondered if the timing was coincidental. "I can't believe we only found one shot of Walter in here. There must be more."

"Let me help." Clay hoped he would find any incriminating photos of Walter with Ruby before Abby did. It would give him the chance to soften the blow. He needed to check records at the courthouse, but he refused to leave Abby just yet.

Two hours later, they'd collectively exhausted every photograph. Alfred left, saying he'd search through the more recent photos he had at home. Now that he had a face to go with the name, he knew who he was looking for.

Abby clipped a leash on Duffy and started for the door. "I need to take him for a walk. Myself, too."

"Mind if I join you?" The courthouse could wait a while longer. "Care to talk about it? I'm a good listener."

"That's funny coming from you," Abby said without looking up. "You're the most closed-off person I know."

"I'm working on changing that, Abby."

"Are you? Because from where I stand, it's hard to tell. One minute you're telling me you want to see where this goes and we're all over each other in your kitchen, and then hours later I don't feel that same connection from you. You run hot and cold. I never know what I'm going to get."

Clay tugged Abby into his arms. "I'm sorry." Tilting her chin toward him, he slanted his mouth over hers for a brief kiss. Abby's arms wound around his waist, pulling him closer.

"I've never been surer of something and more confused at the same time," she whispered.

Clay held her away from him. "Because of me?"

Abby shook her head and began to walk. "That single photograph told me a lot. Mazie said the Harvest Festival always falls on the second weekend in October. I checked the calendar on my phone and that year—the one on the back of the photo—the festival occurred *during* my birthday. Walter was in Ramblewood, three years to the day after I was born. If he didn't have ties to the town, why would he come back? My mom said they lived here for a few months until on-base housing became available. There was something or someone else that brought Walter to Ramblewood. It had to be my sister. One thing bothers me, though."

"What?" Clay feared Abby was connecting the dots to her family tree.

"Why did he come on my birthday and not hers?" Abby asked. "She's here, Clay. I can feel it in my bones."

"Abby—"

"I know it sounds crazy." She quickened her pace and Duffy trotted to keep up. "It's an indescribable feeling, and I've been trying to put my finger on it my entire life. I always felt something was missing. I told myself it was because Wyatt was wholly my parents' child and I was just my mom's…now I know it's more than that. And once again, Walter has sent me on a scavenger hunt for my birthday. Only this time I don't think the prize will necessarily be a happy one all around."

Clay knew exactly what Abby was trying to describe, even if she didn't. He'd read twins had an enormous connection to each other, sometimes even to the extent of feeling the other's pain. If anything, she'd confirmed to him that she didn't know Maeve wasn't her biological mother. If she felt this isolated from her family already, how would she feel when she learned the truth?

He needed to check the records at the courthouse. He

hoped he was wrong. Clay cursed himself for allowing his personal feelings to enter into the equation. Abby Winchester had knocked him off his game from the word go, and now he found himself needing answers fast.

"Let me see what I can dig up," he said. "We have a little more to go on, and there are a few things I want to check out. Will you do something for me in the meantime?"

"What?" Abby hesitantly asked.

"Take a ride out to Dance of Hope. See Kay, play with the dogs, go horseback riding. Get your mind off of this for a while." *And stay the hell away from the center of town.* "Animal therapy is your passion, so take this time to learn everything you can and leave the rest to me. Will you do that?"

Abby regarded him. Worry lines creased her forehead. "I feel like everything is seconds from imploding."

"You need to let me do my job." Clay steered her back in the direction they'd come from. "I'll drive you out there and pick you up later. That way, I won't have to worry about you finding your way back in the dark." Plus, it was the only way he could ensure she stayed away from town and wouldn't accidentally uncover the truth.

"You're right." Abby fell in step beside him. "I do love it out there."

With Abby safely tucked miles away from Bridgett and Ruby, Clay drove to the courthouse. It wasn't legal for him to obtain a copy of Bridgett's birth certificate without a court order, but Clay had a favor or two to call in. As unethical as it was, he convinced himself he was doing it for ethical reasons.

Successful in his quest, he raced home to compare the dates and times on both women's birth certificates. Bridgett's listed her mother as Ruby, the father unknown.

Since Steve Winchester adopted Abby, her parentage had been changed by the state. *Single Birth* was checked on both. Two girls, born on the same day, in the same town, twenty-nine minutes apart.

Under most circumstances, this wouldn't be unusual. Many babies were born around the same time, in the same hospital and no one thought twice about it. But Bridgett's Place of Birth section didn't list a hospital—it had a street address. The Double Trouble ranch. Same as Abby's.

Unless the ranch was a temporary birthing center for one night, Abby and Bridgett were fraternal twins.

Why would Ruby give up one child for adoption and not the other? Did she know she had two babies? If she'd fallen unconscious after delivering the first baby or had been medicated heavily, anything was possible. It was all speculation, but he had to consider every angle.

Stories of baby stealing were sometimes in the news, but in his hometown—on Double Trouble? Maybe he was making too much of this. Grabbing a pad from his kitchen table, he listed the places he needed to investigate next. Newspaper archives for missing baby stories and birth announcements. He'd also check in with the police department. But Clay instinctively knew he'd come up empty-handed.

There were too many factors in play and he'd have to talk to Ruby before he told Abby what he had unearthed. But if his hunches were correct, how would Abby react when she discovered her parents had lied to her since birth. When she had said finding her sister would change her life, she hadn't been kidding. Pandora's box was officially opened. Clay tapped his pen on the table. What about Beau and Mable? What was their role in this?

And Ruby. How did he tell a woman he had found

her secret long-lost daughter? And how could he tell her daughters that they each had a secret twin sister? This was a small town, and he considered Ruby and Bridgett part of his extended family. A heavy feeling settled in his stomach. There was no way to handle this without hurting them.

Clay swung by the Curl Up & Dye first. Shut tighter than a clam with a sore throat, he forgot the salon was always closed on Mondays. He needed answers, and this time he refused to take no for an answer. Beau and Mable had some explaining to do.

From Double Trouble's entrance, Clay saw Beau's truck once again parked at the ranch. Beau stood on the cottage's front porch, talking to Mable.

Clay parked, hopped down from his truck and strode over to the porch stairs.

"Beau, Mable." Clay tipped his hat. "I need to have a word with you both."

Beau didn't make eye contact. Instead, he hastened down the stairs with a speed Clay didn't think the man was capable of at his age.

"Some other time," the man called over his shoulder. "I have business to tend to."

"I know about Bridgett and Abby," Clay called out.

The words hung in the air like a thick black cloud over the two of them. Beau stood frozen, his back to Clay.

"It's time, Beau," Mable said from the top of the porch stairs. Her hands pressed into each other in front of her. She looked skyward, as if she were praying for help.

Beau faced Clay. Lines of worry etched his forehead. "This wasn't supposed to happen. No one was to know."

"Come inside." Mable beckoned them to follow her into the cottage.

The afternoon sun shone through the windows, casting deep shadows across the kitchen. Mable grabbed the percolator from the counter and rinsed it at the sink. She reached into a grape-vine decorated ceramic canister and scooped some fresh ground coffee into the metal basket. Satisfied, she plugged the cord into the pot.

"Don't stand there with your hats in your hands," Mable chastised. "Both of you, sit. Now."

The men did as they were told. No one dared to disobey Mable. She'd threatened to tan plenty of hides in her day.

"Ruby was different back then," Beau began. "She was from Georgia. Married at seventeen to her high school sweetheart and divorced by the time she was nineteen. She wasn't cut out to be a soldier's wife. Randolph Air Force Base was the end of the line for her and her marriage. She played around some. Not a lot, but enough to get herself pregnant."

"Why do men say that?" Mable interrupted. "Women don't get themselves pregnant. It takes two to tango, old man."

"Pardon me." Beau gave Mable's hand a gentle squeeze. "A child didn't fit into Ruby's life. She had plans. Big plans, she used to say, although I can't quite remember what those plans were. Doesn't matter now. Anyway, she arranged to put the baby up for adoption."

"In the meantime," Mable said. "Ruby lived here, at the ranch, with Fran and Ed. They took a liking to her straight away. Not having kids themselves, they treated Ruby as if she were their daughter."

"It still doesn't explain why she gave Abby up for adoption and kept Bridgett," Clay said.

"Ruby never knew she was pregnant with twins," Mable explained. "She didn't have the best medical care and she showed up here somewhere in her eighth month."

"How is that even possible?" Clay asked.

"It wasn't like today where the mothers have all these ultrasounds and 3D imaging. Hell, they know what the baby looks like before God does. The poor girl had nothing."

"Nothing except a set of lungs that were loud enough to wake the dead five counties over." Beau wiped his forehead with a faded blue bandana. "I'll never forget the night those babies were born."

"I was right." Clay slapped the table. "You were there."

"I was a ranch hand at the time." The old man rested against the ladder-back frame of the chair. He smiled across the table at Mable. "Remember how tiny they were?"

"How could I forget? I was the first person on this earth to hold them."

"You?" Clay asked.

"I think Ruby wanted to forget she was pregnant up until the final push. She didn't tell anyone she was in labor until that first baby practically fell out of her. By then it was too late to get her to the hospital. She wouldn't have gone anyway. Couldn't afford it. Plus, she was ashamed she was giving her baby away. No matter how many times we told her there was no shame in making sure her child had a loving home."

"But there were two babies," Clay said.

"I still don't know who was more surprised," Mable said. "Ruby didn't want to see her daughter. She banned her from the room the instant she was born. Fran consoled Ruby while I looked after the baby downstairs until Dr. Barnes arrived."

"Dr. Barnes?"

"You may not remember him," Mable replied. "He retired a year or so later. When we knew it was too late to get Ruby to the hospital, we called him."

"Then the screaming began again," Beau said.

"It sure did," Mable said. "I thought Ruby was dying by the sound of those screams. I handed the baby off to Ed and watched that poor girl writhe in pain, screaming at the top of her lungs. Honey, let me tell you. We were scared and didn't know what was wrong. Until she said she had to push. And she pushed herself out another baby."

Clay raked his hand through his hair. "I saw both birth certificates. They both say single birth. Abby's adoption would have changed her records, but not Bridgett's. Why doesn't hers state she had a twin?"

"Because when Dr. Barnes arrived, he was as surprised as all of us were," Mable said. "I'm not saying it was right, but things were done to keep Ruby's secret. The adoption agency only knew about the one child. Ruby kept the other for herself."

"Why didn't you try to stop her?" Clay demanded.

"It wasn't our place," Beau answered. "This was Ruby's decision. We honored it and we stood beside her. This was her secret, not ours. We kept our promise until you went nosing around."

Stunned to hear the words come from his friend's mouth, Clay stormed out onto the front porch. If he gripped the railing any harder, it would split in two. This wasn't his doing. It was a lie that had taken on a life of its own. And it was about to end. Abby deserved to know who she was.

The screen door squeaked behind him. The featherweight touch of Mable's hand grazed his shoulder.

"Don't jump to too many conclusions, child," the woman soothed. "People have reasons for what they've done. You may not agree with them, but it's not up to us to judge."

"I was paid to do a job, Mable." Clay turned to face her. "Abby hired me to find her sister. For Beau to accuse me of disrupting everyone's life is insulting."

"Beau's upset," Mable said. "He's worried how people are going to take the news. This affects people other than Abby, and you best remember that before you accuse anyone of things you know nothing about. Ruby has to explain all of this to Bridgett. Who I doubt will be none too pleased with Beau and me for keeping this secret all these years. But again, it wasn't our secret to tell. And once word gets out, people will talk and take sides. It's not all about Abby."

"It may not be all about Abby, but it's her life that has been the biggest lie. Her mother isn't her mother. I'm assuming Walter is her father, though."

Mable withdrew her hand. "Honestly, Clay, I have no idea. Ruby wouldn't discuss it."

Anger built deep in Clay's chest. He was about to break Abby's heart in the worst possible way. If you couldn't trust your parents, the ones who should always protect you, who could you trust?

Clay vowed to protect Abby from this point forward. The only way he knew how to ease the blow was for the words to come from Ruby herself. Abby's life, up until now had been one giant lie. A lie her father had tried to explain on his deathbed.

Chapter Eight

Abby was grateful Kay had allowed her to bring Duffy to Dance of Hope. Friskier than usual, her dog trotted in circles in front of her, excited to be in his new favorite surroundings. A trip to the ranch meant playtime with Kay's dog, Barney.

Clay had been right, she felt better already. If she focused on her dreams for the future, the past would fall into place. She had a private investigator on the job and she needed to trust him. Something she had found rather easy to do since the day they'd met.

The Ride 'em High! Rodeo School was in full swing in the outdoor corrals between the arena and the main stables. Teenagers whooped and hollered atop bucking broncos while their instructors coached them from the safety of the fence rails.

Shortening Duffy's leash, Abby walked past the two bronze statues at the entrance to the combined facilities. On the left, a life-size statue of Kay's granddaughter, Ever, perched upon her hippotherapy horse, glinted in the afternoon sun. To the right, a bucking bronco with a twentysomething Joe Langtry, on his final professional ride, cast a larger-than-life shadow against the building's facade.

Abby opened the doors leading into the arena's stone

entryway, which divided the therapy area from the school. Abby didn't think anyone would be inside on such a gorgeous day, but she looked around just in case.

The hippotherapy's massive arena contained smaller sections designated for different types of therapy. One area in particular held a flatbed wagon for patients unable to sit in the saddle. The more Abby studied equine physiology, the more sense the therapy made to her. She'd be forever grateful for the books Kay had loaned her from Joe's personal library on the subject.

Standing at the head of the arena, Abby experienced an air of calmness she didn't feel when working at the hospital. There were certain people who deemed her nothing more than a troublemaker because of the recommendations she made. Then there were others, who commended her initiative.

The Langtrys were progressive. They appreciated an unconventional approach to physical along with cognitive therapy. They provided the type of environment Abby wanted to work in. Despite the details she would need to iron out, each day she spent in town deepened her desire to call Ramblewood home. If only it were that simple.

Leading Duffy through the hallway toward the back door, she exited the building and headed for the outdoor riding area. The complete opposite of the rodeo school's corrals, plenty of trees provided shade in Dance of Hope's secluded area.

Kay sat at a picnic table with a mound of file folders in front of her. She looked up when Abby approached.

"Welcome to my outdoor office. When the weather's this nice, I think it's a sin to stay inside." Kay leaned down and scratched Duffy behind the ears. "And how are you today, little fella? Barney will be thrilled to see you."

"Are you sure it's okay I brought him?" Abby asked. "I know you said it was, but I don't want to impose."

"First of all, you're not imposing. And second, all animals are welcome here anytime."

"Thank you, I appreciate it," Abby said. "I love the serenity here."

"Speaking of love...how's Clay?"

Abby inwardly laughed. The woman deserved credit. She never gave up.

"He's good. I just wish I knew more about him. It's very one-sided. He knows quite a bit about me and I know next to nothing about him."

"I could tell you a million stories from twenty years ago, but I think you're looking for something more recent, and that I can't help you with. Have you tried asking him?"

"No. Everyone's warned me to tread lightly and told me how closed off he is. I didn't want to push the issue, but before the relationship can go any further he needs to open up to me a little more. He dropped me off and said he'll pick me up later."

"That sounds promising." Kay winked.

"And what are you implying?" Abby's voice rose at the woman's insinuation.

Kay smiled and shrugged her shoulders slightly. "Nothing, just that you're both young, available and clearly interested in each other."

"You don't give up, do you?" The warmth that radiated from Kay and the rest of the Langtrys made knowing them for a few days feel more like a lifetime. Abby settled onto the bench across from the woman. "I want you to know that I haven't completely ruled out your job offer. The more I think about it, the more tempted I am.

But there's a lot I would need to work out before I could give you a definitive answer."

"We'd be happy to have you join our extended family. I've considered bringing on another therapist for a while, so please don't think I'm trying to lure you here for any other reason other than I think you'd be a good fit. Clay, well, seeing him happy and settled like most of my boys are would do that man a world of good. His mama would tell you the same. I do hope you get the chance to meet her before you head back to Charleston."

"I'd like that. It would be nice to see where Clay came from."

"Then tell him, Abby." Kay laughed. "These men are a stubborn lot. He was practically raised alongside my boys, and believe me when I say, Clay's no different than they are. Unless it's in black and white, they won't see it."

"I'll take that under advisement." Abby laughed at Kay's honest depiction of her sons and Clay. She'd met too many mothers who thought the sun rose and set on their sons, some of whom were the biggest jackasses she'd had the unfortunate pleasure of knowing. Kay called it as she saw it. "I need to talk to you about a few things, though. In order to consider your offer fully, I have to ask the dreaded money question—not that I'm basing my decision solely on the financial aspect, but it does factor in."

"Of course it does, dear. If you decide to take the job, you'd shadow one of our other therapists until you passed your PATH certification and the Hippotherapy Clinical Specialty Certification examination. Depending on how things go with your horsemanship training, we're probably looking at somewhere around a year before you'd be up to speed. But if you'd be willing to pitch in around here and help with the horses, I'd be able to justify a full-time salary. How about we get this little guy up to the main house to see Barney and we can discuss it further?"

"I also wanted to talk to you about Ruby Jameson," Abby said as they walked toward the house. "I've been working with her on some physical therapy exercises, and from what I can determine so far, the majority of her issues are in her hips and spine. I wondered if she'd be able to have a hippotherapy evaluation, with the understanding that she can't afford to pay for it. She's barely getting by with the salon and the house, since her injury set her back financially. Struggling with her physical recovery is adding more stress to an already stressful situation. But I don't know if she would qualify for financial assistance under your guidelines."

Kay stopped and covered Abby's hand with her own. "Dance of Hope is a nonprofit. If someone needs help, we provide it without financial worry. The donations we receive go toward our patients' care. There are no set guidelines. I run Dance of Hope to help people and fulfill my husband's vision. We would be more than happy to evaluate Ruby."

"Thank you." The constant insurance battles at the hospital often meant Abby's patients were forced to leave without fully recovering. "I mentioned it in passing to Bridgett to gauge how her mother would feel about my asking and she thinks Ruby would love the idea."

"I know she's had a tough time since her accident, and I'm ashamed for not suggesting it myself."

"Don't be," Abby said. "When Ruby told me how she broke her leg, I honestly thought her pain was more of an issue of the bone healing incorrectly. I looked at her records and X-rays, and it's not. Ruby stayed on top of her physical therapy, but she ran out of money and the insurance will only pay so much."

"Most insurance won't cover hippotherapy anyway. That's the main reason a facility like ours was so important to my husband. He believed people deserved to get the help they needed, without any undue burden."

"Whatever my reasons for coming to Ramblewood were, I'm glad I met you and your family," Abby said. "You've expanded my outlook on animal-assisted therapy."

"Still no luck with finding your sister?" Kay asked, opening the gate to her side yard. "Look who's here to see you, Barney."

Abby removed Duffy's harness and leash, allowing him to run free with his playmate.

"Clay told me a few days ago he felt my suspicions were spot on, but he wouldn't elaborate. He also told me that if my sister did not want to be found he'd need to respect her wishes and not give me the contact information."

"That must've been disheartening to hear."

"To say the least. I once wondered—if I located her, would she want anything to do with me? I never thought we might never have that conversation. I figured I'd pay Clay, and wherever she turned up I'd be able to talk to her."

"I can understand the logic behind that," Kay said. "If you look at it from her perspective, what if she's hiding for some reason? Maybe there's an explanation why she stayed away from you, or your father, if she even knew about you."

"That's basically what Clay said. When I asked if it was the law that he couldn't tell me, he told me it came down to ethics. And I understand his position. As a physical therapist I make those decisions about my patients daily, and some are harder than others. Just last week I had to call child protective services on a parent of an out-patient because the bruises on the child's body seemed excessive for someone recovering from leg surgery. The parent was the only family in the child's life. When I made the call, I was potentially tearing his life apart, but I had to put the child's safety first. Whatever the outcome is with my sister, I'll accept it."

Abby no longer doubted the possibility of a sister. She only hoped that once her sister was located, she'd be as thrilled to meet Abby as Abby was to meet her. Where she used to be nervous about what Clay might unearth, after seeing the photo of Walter in town, excitement had begun to replace the uncertainty about knowing the truth. She finally allowed herself to wonder about her sister's life. Maybe she had children and a husband…an entire family for Abby to meet.

CLAY WAS TICKED he'd been unable to get hold of Ruby, forcing him to wait until tomorrow. When he couldn't locate her anywhere in town, he had his suspicions that Beau or Mable had warned her and she was avoiding him. It was late and he needed to pick up Abby from the Langtrys before she made her way back into town with one of them and stumbled upon the truth. Any time she now spent with Bridgett was akin to playing a game of catch with a ticking time bomb. All it would take is a mention of their upcoming birthdays and he didn't want Abby to find out that way.

"How the hell am I going to keep her occupied for the rest of the night?"

The weather was still warm enough for a drive-in movie in the next town over, but Clay wasn't sure which risk was worse. Abby talking to Bridgett or him spending time alone with Abby in the darkness of his truck's cab.

Clay called Abby to say he was on the way. He pulled into Bridle Dance's main ranch road and saw Abby hugging Kay goodbye on the front porch of the main house.

"Hey, stranger." Abby lifted Duffy into his truck and climbed in after him. "How was your afternoon?"

"Apparently not as good as yours." Abby's smile radiated straight to his heart. It was a smile he could build a universe around and create his own orbit. He wanted to kiss her hello and ask her never to leave town, regardless of what she discovered about her family. "You look a lot better than you did when I dropped you off."

"I feel better," Abby said. "Kay and I had a long talk about the possibility of my working at Dance of Hope, and I'm seriously giving it more thought. The search for my sister aside, the likelihood that Walter knew about Dance of Hope is high. Ramblewood is too small a town for him not to. I think it may have been part of his plan all along. I'm beginning to believe Ramblewood is the answer to more than one question." She rested her hand on his. "And however you factor into the equation, I'm glad I met you."

Her touch was almost unbearable as guilt swept through him like an icy February breeze. He wanted to tell her the truth. To tell her she was right and there was much more to Walter's note than just her finding her sister, but not quite the way she thought. Clay's heartbeat hammered in his ears as he struggled with the right words to say when something suddenly flopped against his hip. He peered down to see Duffy staring up at him with watchful eyes. Abby's therapy dog was about to give him away. Apparently, Clay had a tell or two of his own that only the dog could detect. He was learning fast not to underestimate the power of a canine's perception.

"How do you feel about a drive-in movie tonight?"

"They still have those around here?" Abby's voice hitched. "I'd love to go. I've never been to one."

"Really?" The unexpected thrill of taking Abby to her first drive-in caught him off guard. "It would be my pleasure to be your first."

"Why, Clay Tanner, I do believe you're flirting with me." Abby batted her eyelashes at him.

"I do believe I am, Miss Winchester." Clay attempted to bow across the seat only to receive a tongue bath from Duffy. "Thanks, pal."

Abby giggled. "I think he likes you. I need to stop by the Bed & Biscuit to feed him." Abby scratched her companion on the top of his head. "Are dogs allowed at the drive-in?"

Clay figured a four-legged chaperone was probably a good idea. The dog's internal barometer would keep Clay's conscience in check along with his mounting libido.

"I think we can manage to sneak him in." Clay watched Duffy's ears perk up as if he understood what they were talking about. "He doesn't seem to be much of a barker, so I don't think he'll give us away."

"Oh, he barks...at dogs on TV, squirrels in the yard, and heaven forbid a dog walks past his Mini Cooper. Then all hell breaks loose."

"His Mini Cooper?" Clay laughed. "Now I've heard it all."

"Didn't you know?" Abby furrowed her brow. "I'm just the maid. The dog rules the roost."

Two hours later, Clay found his fingers entwined with Abby's and his arm wrapped around her shoulder while Duffy snored the night away on the passenger side of the truck. So much for a chaperone.

Clay attempted to mentally drive the tension from his body. Between the side of Abby's breast bouncing against him every time she laughed at the movie and knowing the truth about Bridgett, Clay couldn't clench his jaw any tighter or he'd chip a tooth.

"Are you feeling okay?" Abby looked up at him.

"Yeah, why?" Clay's throat thickened.

"You feel extremely hard." Abby closed her eyes. "That didn't quite come out the way I intended."

Clay grinned. Even in the dim light from the movie screen, he saw a flush fan across her cheeks.

"Well, darlin', maybe that's the problem," Clay teased.

"Oh, really?" Abby sat straighter, angling toward him. "I thought after our little tryst in your kitchen that you wanted to cool things."

"I wanted to slow down a little before we couldn't stop what we were doing. I don't know whatever gave you the impression I wanted to cool things. I'm as attracted to you now as I was before. For the record, I've never been one of those *wham, bam, thank you, ma'am* types. I like to romance a woman."

Clay tried to push the memory of his last date with Ana Rosa out of his head. He didn't want to feel the ever-present guilt. Not tonight. While it had faded some, it was still there. And now, with Abby by his side, was not the time to remember what he'd had and lost. He wanted to enjoy feeling alive again.

"You know what I think is romantic?" Abby ever-so-slightly chewed on her bottom lip.

"Do I dare ask?" Clay leaned closer.

"Go ahead," Abby whispered.

"What do you find romantic?"

"I've always wanted to make out at a drive-in movie."

"Then who am I to deny your desires?"

Clay drew Abby tight to his chest. There was no accidental brush of her breast against him. This time, she full-on flattened her upper body against his chest and Clay enjoyed every minute of it. Heaven have mercy.

Pushing whatever guilt he felt earlier to the back of his mind, Clay reveled in having Abby alone to himself…in his arms, where she belonged. After she discovered the truth, he may never have the chance again. Tonight might be all they would have, and Clay wasn't about to let what may be a once-in-a-lifetime opportunity pass him by.

"First, I served Clay alone yesterday and then you today." Bridgett flipped over Abby's coffee cup and filled it. "What's up with you two?"

"I saw him last night," Abby began, opting not to share the details of their drive-in excursion. They had missed the end of the movie, which was okay with her. She'd rather steam up the windows in the cab of a pickup truck than watch a stale old movie any day. "I have so much to tell you about my search. Alfred Anderson had a photo of Walter that was taken when I was about three. There was only one, but he was with the mayor."

"Darren Fox?" Bridgett asked. "Maybe he'll know something."

"Clay said he'd talk to Darren when he returns from some fishing trip."

"I don't know what I would do if I were in your shoes. I guess I'd want to know, but I'd always wonder why it was a secret in the first place. Was it because of me or them?"

"Believe me, I've asked a million questions and received zero answers." Abby sighed. "It's heartbreaking. I've always wanted kids of my own, and I could never imagine keeping them from one another. My dad—stepdad—is wonderful, but Wyatt and my parents are the family unit. I'm the outsider looking in. That's how I feel, anyway. To know I had a sister out there all these years and didn't know it is almost inconceivable. We were both short-changed years that we can never get back."

"Maybe there's a good reason for all of this," Bridgett reassured her.

"That's what I keep telling myself. I've had my entire life mapped out since I was a little girl. Followed it to the letter, yet somehow it's still empty. Now I feel my career may be veering down a parallel path, and I'm beginning to wonder if Dance of Hope is the brass ring. I tell my patients to live every day to the fullest. I think it's time I started following my own advice. Even though I've attempted to attain my goals, maybe Charleston was the wrong place."

"Order up," Bert called from the kitchen pass-through window.

Bridgett glanced over her shoulder. "Give me a minute and I'll be back."

"No, go." Abby shooed Bridgett away. "I'm good with coffee. You're busy."

Abby watched Bridgett hurry around the luncheonette. It definitely paid to have a mother who owned a salon. If Abby had half of Bridgett's beauty, she'd be satisfied.

Since she had time to spare this morning, Abby decided to pop across the street and see if she could get her hair trimmed. She had a feeling things with Clay were close to progressing to the *see-me-naked* stage and she could stand some head-to-toe primping.

WHEN CLAY DROVE past the Curl Up & Dye salon, the last thing he expected to see was Abby sitting in the front window with Ruby.

He slapped the steering wheel before making a sharp impromptu turn in the middle of Main Street.

"Why can't she stay out of the damn salon?"

Because Ruby's her mother.

Jamming his truck into Park, Clay ran to the salon, almost tearing the door off the hinges as he stormed in.

"Clay!" Shock registered on Abby's face. "What's wrong?"

"Ruby." Clay crossed the room in four long strides. "I need to talk to you about that matter you asked me to look into the other day."

Clay motioned toward the back office, but the woman didn't take the hint.

"What matter?" she questioned. "I didn't ask you to—"

"Yes, you did, Ruby." Clay lightly gripped her arm and tugged her up from her chair. "I know you don't want to discuss this in public."

Still confused, she allowed Clay to lead her to the salon office.

"Clay!" Ruby shrugged out of his grip. "What is wrong with you?"

"Don't tell me you don't know who that is," Clay said.

Ruby tilted her head. "That's Abby Winchester."

"Care to expand on that?"

"I—I don't know what you're talking about." Ruby turned away, her shoulders trembling.

"Ruby." Clay gently touched her arm in an attempt to get her to face him. She shook her head, as if willing away what he was about to say. "I know the truth. You know she hired me to find her sister. Did you really think I wouldn't find out?"

"Find out what?" Ruby began to sort through papers on her desk.

"Ruby, Abby is your biological daughter." There was no candy-coating the words. He needed her attention.

The woman's legs gave out and Clay caught her before she hit the floor. Guiding Ruby to a chair, he held her hand as she leaned forward and sobbed.

"When Abby first showed up, I didn't think anything of it," Ruby confessed, after she stopped hyperventilating. "It wasn't until after Bridgett told me Abby was in town looking for her sister that I thought it was possible. The other day, when I saw them side by side, I knew... I just knew she was my daughter. And I was okay with it. I had covered my tracks. I figured she'd find nothing and leave town, but at least I finally knew what became of my daughter."

"Ruby." Clay crouched in front of her. "I'm giving you the chance to tell Bridgett and Abby yourself. Bridgett especially needs to hear this from you. If I tell Abby, she's going to run straight to Bridgett and you don't want that."

"Please give me a few days," Ruby pleaded, tears streaming down her face. "I need to figure out a way to tell them."

Clay hated lying to Abby. He'd planned to give Ruby only a couple of hours to tell her daughters the truth, not days. After last night, he refused to keep this secret from Abby. He knew it wasn't his place, but ethics be damned, he wasn't going lie to Abby much longer. His heart couldn't take it.

"I'll give you forty-eight hours, Ruby, but that's it." Clay rose. "Don't take advantage of my good nature on this one. A woman's life is about to be drastically changed with this information. She deserves to know the truth. At least Bridgett knows you're her mother, Abby doesn't have a clue."

"I—I understand," Ruby stammered.

"In the meantime, I need to find a way to keep Abby away from you and Bridgett."

"Why?" Ruby's voice pitched high.

"Those girls are a hairsbreadth away from finding out they're sisters. They have a birthday in a few weeks. That's bound to come up in conversation. I'm actually surprised it hasn't already. Why didn't you ask Abby her birthday? That would've answered your question from the beginning."

"Because I didn't want to know. I liked the idea of knowing, but I hated the certainty. I always wondered how my daughter turned out. If she had a good life. I had a fantasy of what became of her. I know this doesn't make any sense to you, but I told myself that if Abby was my daughter then I made the right decision by giving her away. Look at the life she's had!"

"And look at the life she missed out on," Clay argued. "Ruby, I'm not judging you. I'm worried about Abby. No matter how you spin this, and regardless of how wonderful you think Abby's life has been, the fact remains that her entire life has been a lie. The guilt she carries for not being there when Walter died is bad enough. Now she'll learn her mother isn't really her mother. She already feels like an outsider in her family because her mother and stepfather have a son of their own. Imagine how she's going to feel now."

"I never thought her parents would keep her adoption from her," Ruby argued. "Don't you dare lay that part on me. That's on them."

"No one could have predicted how this would turn out. If you want a relationship with Abby, the only way is to tell her the truth. Beau and Mable said you thought you were doing the honorable thing. I'm sure none of this was easy for you."

"Beau and Mable?" Ruby's lips thinned.

"Don't be mad at them, Ruby." Clay's neck stiffened. How could Ruby be more concerned with whether or not her friends had betrayed her than what her daughters' reactions to the truth might be. "They didn't have any choice in the matter. I had figured it out. I just needed them to confirm the facts."

Tears filled Ruby's eyes. "Please don't think any less of me for what I did."

"I've no right judge you. But when you tell Abby, I want to be there. You're going to have your hands full supporting Bridgett, and I'll be there for Abby. This can't drag out, though. I don't want to give you a couple of days, but I will. I have to tell Abby she's adopted. I don't have to tell her that you're her mother, but she's going to ask, and this puts me in a terrible position."

"Understood." Ruby nodded and walked unsteadily toward the back door of the salon. Opening it, she poked her head out and looked in both directions. "I don't want anyone to see me this way. Would you please tell everyone up front I had to leave?"

"Fine. What do you want me to say?"

"I don't know… Say I received a phone call while we were talking and someone's having a hair emergency."

"A hair emergency?" That was a new one.

"It happens more often than you realize. Especially when people attempt to color their own hair. Please do this for me."

Clay bobbed his head in agreement and Ruby grabbed her purse, practically running out the back door. Rubbing his eyes with his palms, Clay didn't know how he'd keep the truth from Abby. How the hell was he going to keep her away from the center of town? He had his work cut out for him, considering she stayed across the street at the Bed & Biscuit.

He inhaled deeply then emerged from the salon's office.

"Is everything okay?" Abby asked. "Where's Ruby?"

"Hair emergency, if you can believe that." Clay rolled his eyes. "Someone called—something about coloring their own hair and they had problems. Ruby took off."

"Oh, I can see how that would happen," Abby said. "I remember the time I darkened my hair and it turned an eggplant color. That was definitely a hair emergency. I sympathize with whoever it was."

Clay couldn't imagine that what he had thought was a ridiculous cover story had actually happened. Why couldn't women leave well enough alone and keep their natural hair color?

"In the meantime, I'm available this afternoon if you'd like another riding lesson."

"I'd love to, but I was planning on going to Dance of Hope. I really need to spend as much time there as possible if I'm to give Kay's job offer my full consideration."

Hearing Abby reiterate her interest in Dance of Hope should have made him the happiest man on earth, but not when it was clouded in so many lies. "How about we meet for dinner tonight?"

Hard as it was being around Abby and not telling her the truth, he knew if he didn't tie up her schedule, chances were she'd spend time with Bridgett. Their fast friendship made perfect sense now.

"Sure, dinner sounds wonderful. I'll call you after I'm through at the ranch and we'll set a time."

"Let me walk you out." Clay wasn't taking any chances on Abby veering toward The Magpie for a gossip fest with Bridgett.

He held the door of the salon open for her.

Abby swatted his arm. "You don't have to walk me home, Clay. I can manage to cross the street by myself." She gave him a quick kiss on the cheek. "I'll see you later."

This simple gesture made him feel like a first-class ass. He'd managed to block her schedule for tonight, but, come tomorrow, he didn't know how he'd continue to lie to her: This is exactly why he should never get involved with a client.

Especially one he was falling in love with.

Chapter Nine

"Are you sure you don't want to go someplace else?" Clay asked Abby a few hours later as he opened the door to The Dog House.

"Not at all." Abby slipped under his arm and inside. "I love street food. Every time I take Duffy to the Bark Park I can smell these hot dogs. I've been dying for one since I got here. And don't try to pay for mine, because I'm treating you this time."

Inside the brightly lit red-and-yellow take-out restaurant, they ordered a couple of fully loaded hot dogs, nachos and a pretzel the size of Abby's head.

They carried their food outside then made the short five-minute walk around the corner to the large recreational park, which boasted picnic tables and an athletic track. They spread their meal on one of the tables.

"I can't believe you're going to eat all of that," Clay said.

"I have a very healthy appetite, but if I don't start working out again, I'm going to be in some serious trouble. I haven't burned off a single thing I've eaten since I came here. Hey, you haven't noticed my new boots."

"No, you're right, I haven't. How very manly of me not to." Clay attempted to talk his way out of his oversight. "What, no pink cowboy boots? Were they out of fringe?"

"I can be conservative when I need to be." Abby lifted her chin. "Besides, the fringed ones didn't come in my size and Bridgett told me they would probably get caught in the stirrups."

"Bridgett would be correct." Clay cringed at the mention of her name. Bridgett's father had never been around. Her birth certificate stated *unknown* in the paternity section. What lie had Ruby told to cover Bridgett's absent father?

"Hello, earth to Clay." Abby waved her hand in front of him. "Where did you go just now?"

"Sorry, I was thinking about a case." Clay wanted to direct the conversation away from Abby's search. He hated lying to her. She deserved to know she was adopted, but he understood why Ruby needed some time to figure out how to break the news to Bridgett. Plus, in his heart, Clay knew once Abby found out, she'd leave town…and him.

"My case?" Abby sighed. "You found her, didn't you? And you're trying to convince her to meet with me."

Something like that.

"Abby, let's wait another day or two and see what happens."

"I'm right, aren't I? You do know who my sister is." She rewrapped her hot dog and shoved it into the paper sack.

"Abby, there are a lot of things I'm not sure of." That much wasn't a lie. "I hope to learn more in a couple of days. Please grant me that much. I don't have all the answers yet, but I'm working on it."

"I'm sorry. It's hard not to ask you a million questions right now. I guess this goes back to what you were saying about mixing business with pleasure."

"It does," Clay agreed. "But it's too late for that now.

I'm already involved, and hopefully that won't change. Trust me, please."

He feared there was the real possibility that once Abby found out who her sister and mother were she'd want no further part of Ramblewood. On the flipside, maybe she'd want to stay and get to know Bridgett and Ruby better.

"Fine." Abby removed her hot dog from the sack and unwrapped it for the second time. "I had another long talk with Kay today. I'm not saying yes yet, but I'm leaning more toward moving to Ramblewood. Before I make my final decision, I would like to speak with the hospital board in Charleston again. I think I owe them that courtesy. My patients deserve the best care they can get, and if my head's not a hundred percent in the game, then I need to be where it will be."

"You've fit in very nicely here." Clay cursed his silent prayer for her to stay. It no longer mattered what he wanted. Or what she wanted. In less than two days, her life would change dramatically, along with her priorities. His instinct was to protect her, but in reality, he couldn't. Her happiness was all he cared about, and if they had only the next few days together, he'd make the best of them. "Heck, even I've taken a likin' to ya."

Abby playfully kicked at him under the table. A cool evening breeze rustled the wax paper beneath their dinner. A wisp of hair crossed her cheek and he was thankful she pushed it aside before he could—he would have been unable to resist kissing her.

"Tell me something I don't know about you." Clay needed to learn everything possible about the woman sitting across from him.

Abby laughed. "You ran the background check on me. Don't you know already?"

"I made sure you weren't a criminal." He winked.

"But I didn't pull your whole life history. Tell me about your parents."

"Mom and Dad live in Altoona, Pennsylvania. My father's a stockbroker and my mother is a party planner. They've both done very well for themselves and travel extensively throughout the world whenever they can."

"Why didn't you fly to Texas instead of driving all that way by yourself?"

"I don't fly or take trains," Abby stated flatly.

"I've heard of a fear of flying, but a fear of trains?"

"You never know when a random cow is going to wander onto the tracks and cause a derailment. I've seen it on the news. No, thank you. Driving is my only option."

"I'm sensing a pattern." Clay picked up a gooey nacho and devoured it in one bite. "Let me guess, you have a fear of cruises, too."

"Cruise ships are a hotbed of diseases." Abby handed him a napkin when the cheese ran down his chin. "There's no safe way of eating any of this, is there?"

"How did you end up in Charleston?"

"There were two hospitals that offered me a residency. I chose the one without snow. Charleston is a magnificently historical city and its charm won me over."

"Yet, you're willing to leave it?" Clay questioned.

"I think maybe it's time." Abby sighed. "My turn, because I barely know a thing about you. If you weren't a private investigator, what other profession do you see yourself in?"

"That's easy. I'd own an alpaca farm." Clay sipped his soda. "Those were my plans when I bought the ranch. My parents, grandparents and great-grandparents were sheep farmers, and when I was in college, the business went bankrupt. My plans were, and still are, if I can ever find the time, to start an alpaca farm and bring my dad in on it."

"I love alpacas," Abby exclaimed.

"What does a cultured city girl want with an alpaca?" Clay couldn't envision her shearing the animal. Then again, nothing she did would surprise him.

"Alpaca fleece is amazingly warm," Abby enthused. "A few years ago, when I was home for Christmas, an ice storm knocked out our power for days. Our alpaca blankets kept us nice and toasty. Even our dogs have their own. Crap." She dabbed at a spot of cheese on her shirt. "I think I'm managing to wear most of this meal."

Clay handed her another napkin. "My idea is to process the fiber on-site like we used to with the sheep. My father currently manages a fiber mill, and I know every day is a reminder of what he lost. It would take some time to get the mill up and running, but I think it would be well worth it."

"Definitely. When I stopped in The Knitters Circle the other day, I asked if they had any alpaca yarn and they didn't. It's a hot commodity. Do you know how much money you could make with alpacas? The price of alpaca yarn is higher than your standard wool, which is prickly to wear and work with. Plus, wool tends to bother me because I'm sensitive to lanolin. Never mind that alpaca fiber is naturally water repellent, making it even more desirable."

"You knit?" Clay tried to picture Abby sitting in a rocking chair, working two knitting needles as his grandmother did. It seemed far-fetched. Even for her.

"Are you kidding me? Knitting is the *in* thing. Everyone does it. Although my friend Amanda is so awkward with the needles, she almost gouges her eye out every time."

Clay laughed at the visual Abby described. "Getting the business running is a big process." He sighed. "It's not like I have the time."

"You have the land and it's my understanding alpacas are fairly easy to take care of. Yes, you'd probably need some help, but if I move to town, I'd be willing to get my hands dirty with you. Especially for the chance to spin my own virgin alpaca yarn."

"Have you ever spun yarn?" At this point, Clay wouldn't be surprised to hear Abby spun hay into gold. "It's a tedious process."

"No, but it's something I've always wanted to learn. I go through so much yarn that I'd love to spin my own. That's a dream of mine, and don't you laugh, either."

He held up his hands, knowing well enough never to mess with a woman and her yarn. He had learned that lesson the hard way as a kid. He'd gotten tangled up in his mother's knitting only once, and he'd never done it again.

"I'm sure my mom would love to teach you to spin. She has an antique spinning wheel that she still uses. My parents have only a couple sheep now, but Mom still gets out there and shears them."

Clay's heart pounded harder with each word he spoke. He'd shared his vision with Shane and mentioned it to his father in passing, but it had always seemed more of a dream than a real possibility. Abby made it sound feasible. Why was he waiting to do what he'd planned to do three years ago? With Abby by his side, Clay suspected there'd be no end to what he could accomplish.

"Why don't we find a nearby alpaca ranch and take a little road trip?" Abby wiped off her fingers and pulled her phone from her bag. "This is Texas. They have a ranch for everything, I bet there's one close to here."

If there was ever a perfect chance to spend more time

with Abby and get her away from Ramblewood, then an alpaca ranch was the way.

"Sure, why not? I need to update my research, anyway."

Abby tapped on her phone's screen. "There's one an hour from here. How about tomorrow?"

"It can't be first thing in the morning. A rancher's work is never done and I'm only one person with many mouths to feed and water. I have some fencing to mend on one of the corrals before I move the goats. Even a small herd like mine needs to be on the move so they can graze, plus it helps keep my land from becoming overgrown." His shoulders slumped. "And the roof on the pigpen is about to fall in. I also have a daily manure delivery to make to my neighbor. He's an organic farmer and the easiest way for me to dispose of mine is to sell it to him. How about late morning?"

"I can help you, if you'd like."

"Shovel manure? Gather eggs from ornery chickens? I'm not saying you can't handle the work, I'm just saying ranching is a dirty job."

"I'm not afraid to get dirty, Clay." Abby's face was full of strength and determination.

A new and unexpected warmth surged through him as he envisioned Abby working beside him on his ranch.

"I appreciate the offer, and if you move to Ramblewood then I might just take you up on it, but for now, you are a guest whenever you visit my ranch. All I ask of you is to see if you can arrange our visit tomorrow. We can't just show up unexpectedly. I wouldn't want a stranger driving onto my ranch asking for a tour without calling ahead. Figure we'll be there around one."

"I am so excited. I can't wait to hug an alpaca."

Clay almost choked on his soda. "Abby, you can't just run up and hug one."

"Sure you can." Her thumbs typed wildly on her phone's miniature keyboard. "Look."

Abby handed Clay her phone. On the screen was photo after photo of people hugging alpacas.

"People actually do that? Well, then, alpaca hugging we will go." The words, as corny as they sounded coming from his mouth, made him smile. Alpaca ranching may be a serious dream for Clay, but Abby reminded him not to take it or life too seriously. Something he'd been doing far too much of lately. It had never been something he could discuss with Ana Rosa for fear it would blow his cover. Paulo would've loved it. Ana Rosa he wasn't so sure about. Somehow, the image of them on an alpaca ranch didn't fit as well as it did with Abby. He easily envisioned her there by his side.

"Who knows," Abby said. "Maybe your dreams will come true on this trip."

Clay regarded her across the table. If only she knew how deep his dreams ran and the part she played in them. Closing his eyes, he wanted to commit this moment to memory before everything changed.

THE FOLLOWING MORNING, Abby swung by Clay's ranch to see if they were still on schedule. She knew she could've called, but she wanted to see the man at work, in his natural environment, not all showered and clean as usual.

"I made arrangements for our alpaca tour." Abby opened the gate to the goat pen and slipped in beside Clay, helping him empty one of the water troughs. "I also booked a spa appointment for Duffy."

"Wait, what?" Clay straightened the trough, his arms covered in dirt and dust, sweat trickling down his neck, a formerly white shirt clinging to his body with perspi-ration. *Good God.* He was one hundred percent rugged male and the new sight gave her a better appreciation for how hard he worked. "A spa appointment for the dog?"

"Dogs needed to get beautified, too." Mazie had bragged about Penny's Poodle Parlor, and after reading their menu of services Abby had figured it would be a nice place for Duffy to spend part of the day while she and Clay visited the alpacas.

"If you say so." Clay shook his head. "What time do you want me to swing by and get you?"

"I'll pick you up after I drop him off. Say around noon?"

"Abby." Clay laughed. "I'm six foot five. I can't fit in your car."

"Sure you can." Abby exited the pen. "Trust me. I'll see you a little later." She fought a smile as she pictured Clay getting into her car.

A few hours later, Abby dropped Duffy off at Penny's Poodle Parlor, confident he would have a good time, de-spite his bath and haircut. Penny had a stunning black-and-white parti-poodle named Bella that Duffy fell in love with instantly. The upstairs was an entire playroom devoted to dogs.

Abby pulled alongside Clay's house a short time later. She released the lever under the Mini's passenger seat, allowing it to slide backward.

"I'm not going to fit." Clay poked his head through the sunroof, and Abby inhaled the fresh scent of Ivory soap. "My belt comes up to your roofline. I can literally step into your car through the sunroof."

"Don't you dare," Abby warned. "Stop squawking and get in the car. We're going to be late."

Clay opened the door. "Do the alpacas have some place to be?"

"Ha-ha. Get in."

Clay practically fell in, forcing Abby to hide her laughter.

"How does this thing make it over speed bumps?" He swung his legs inside.

"It doesn't always. I got stuck on a big one once and my car became a teeter-totter. Luckily, some teenagers felt sorry for me and lifted me off it. But don't be fooled, it's far from being a lightweight car. Close the door already."

Clay reached for the handle and eased the door shut. "Hmm."

"Hmm, what?" Abby asked.

"It's actually pretty roomy in here." Clay glanced around. "I wouldn't want to be in the backseat, but this works."

"I'm so glad you approve of my car." Abby smirked and backed out of the driveway.

"My apologies." Clay leaned over the seat and kissed her on the cheek. "Did you ever play rapid fire as a kid?"

"No, what is it?" Abby giggled. "Do I want to know?"

"Usually, you have more than two people, but this will work." Clay reached out and entwined his fingers with Abby's. "I first played it when I was in a church youth group. It's a series of rapid questions. I ask one, you answer, then you fire back one of your own. It's a getting-to-know-you type of game."

"Sure. Fire away, cowboy." Abby stole a glance in his direction.

"Rancher," Clay corrected.

"What's the difference? The Langtrys don't have cows and they're cowboys."

"I just never thought of myself as one. I was never in the rodeo like they were, and while Dream Catcher is *technically* a cutting horse, I only ride him as one when I'm actually helping another rancher move cattle."

"So that would *technically* make you a cowboy." Abby smiled. "But, okay, rancher it is."

"Favorite board game?"

"Clue," Abby answered. "Favorite movie?"

"*Die Hard With a Vengeance*. Stop snorting over there. Favorite sport?"

"Hockey. Favorite—"

"You're a hockey fan?" Clay interrupted. "Who's your team?"

"You'd think I'd be a Penguins or Flyers fan because I'm from Pennsylvania, but I'm a New Jersey Devils fan."

"Yep, that fits you." Clay chuckled. "I'm a Dallas Stars fan. We'll have to watch a game sometime."

"All right, but I'm warning you, I'm one of those loud sports fanatics who yells at the television. So bring your ear plugs. My turn still, favorite book?"

"*To Kill a Mockingbird,*" Clay replied. "Children?"

The question startled Abby. "Is this part of the game?" She looked at Clay and saw him waiting for her answer. "I'd love a houseful of them. More so now that I've spent time in Ramblewood. It's not as affordable in Charleston and…I don't know, the wide-open space here screams for a big family. A family I could actually call my own, without feeling as if I was on the outside looking in. You?"

Clay tightened his hand over hers. "I've always wanted children. It didn't work out that way—"

"Yet."

Clay sheepishly grinned at her, and for a split second, Abby easily pictured what he had looked like as a child. She wondered what their children would look like.

Whoa. She was getting way ahead of herself. She may be contemplating moving to Texas, but it was not to move in with Clay. She'd live—where? When she considered moving to Ramblewood she always pictured she'd be— *with Clay.*

They continued firing questions back and forth until they pulled into the alpaca ranch. Clay was surprised to learn Abby loved football as well as hockey and could climb a gym rope faster than most men.

"Look at them." Clay leaned out the window.

Lush rolling hills were dotted with white, chocolate-and-gold-colored alpacas. Their big watchful eyes followed the Mini as they drove down the farm's dirt road. A handful of Great Pyrenees dogs roamed alongside the younger alpacas.

"Can you envision this on your ranch?" Abby asked.

He could. With Abby by his side he could envision many things.

"Welcome to RJ's Alpacas." A man greeted them in the parking lot. "You must be Abby and Clay. I'm Bob, and you're just in time."

"Just in time for what?" Clay asked, shaking Bob's hand.

"My wife and I are testing to see if one of our females is pregnant. Follow me, but stand back."

Clay wasn't sure what to expect, and neither was Abby judging by the way she tucked herself behind him as they headed for a metal barn.

Bob opened a door and led them into a room. "Stand over in that far corner. You should be out of spit range. I'll be back in a minute."

Clay raised his eyebrows at Abby and she giggled.

"Hello," a woman said from behind a metal fence. Next to her stood a chocolate alpaca, wearing a halter with a lead rope attached to it. "I'm Joan, Bob's wife, and this here is Felicia. The way we test to see if a female's pregnant is by what is known as the *spit test*. Bob's going to bring in a male, and if Felicia's receptive to him, we'll know she's not pregnant. If she spits, then it's a warning sign for him to stay away and we'll soon have a little *cria* running around. A *cria* is a baby alpaca."

"How long is their gestation?" Abby asked from the safety of the corner.

"Eleven months. Usually a single birth." Joan looked up as the door opened. "Here we go. Stay against the wall. Bob is bringing in a *macho*, or a male alpaca, and—" Joan ducked out of Felicia's way as she fired off a spray of spit.

"Oh, my God!" Abby shrieked and gripped Clay's arm tightly. "Did you see that?"

Bob attempted to present the *macho* to Felicia again, but she quickly spit in its face.

"Oh!" Abby cried.

"She can really hock it up, can't she?" Clay laughed.

"She's definitely pregnant, Bob." Joan ducked her head again as Felicia fired another spit attack.

Bob led the *macho* outside and Joan proceeded to wipe off her arm.

"That's how you tell if a *hembra* is pregnant." Joan handed off Felicia to Bob when he returned. Joan unzipped and removed her jacket. "I'd shake your hands, but I think you'd rather pass. Follow me and I'll take you on a tour."

Joan led them to a four-seater John Deere Gator. Allowing Abby to sit up front, Clay climbed in behind her and enjoyed her enthusiasm as they began to move. He laughed quietly to himself, betting she didn't have much of an opportunity to ride a utility vehicle while she was working inside a hospital all day.

The thought of Abby working indoors struck him as odd. Since the day he'd met her, she had seemed more the outdoorsy type. He imagined her smile wouldn't shine as brightly as it did now if she were inside a stuffy hospital.

"How many alpacas do you have?" Abby asked.

"Forty-three." Joan slowed the Gator. "We raise Hua-cayas to breed as well as for their fiber. Alpaca fleece is virtually indestructible. Garments dating back thousands of years have been discovered in ruins throughout Peru."

"When do you shear them?" Abby asked.

"In the spring. Same as sheep. It's a big job and we bring in professional shearers. We don't have the experience to attempt it ourselves. An alpaca needs to be sheared a certain way to get the most out of their fibers." Joan turned her attention to Clay. "I understand from my husband that your family used to own the sheep farm over in Ramblewood. I can remember going there twenty years ago, give or take a few. Quite an operation you had."

Clay blinked, surprised to hear Joan knew who his family was, let alone had met his mother. He looked to Abby who mouthed *sorry.* He smiled and shook his head slightly.

"I'm glad you enjoyed the experience," he said. "I'd like to do the same thing with alpacas, processing our own fiber, on a much smaller scale than my family had, but the same concept."

"You'd fare very well in today's market. American fiber is at a premium."

"Do you process your own fiber?" Abby asked. "I've always wanted to spin my own."

"Some of it. The rest I have processed by a mini-mill. From shearing to yarn is a lengthy process, but I recommend it to anyone who loves to knit. It's a rewarding experience."

Clay bet Abby was taking mental notes on every word out of Joan's mouth. Glancing around, he imagined what it would be like to run his own alpaca ranch. He was already devoting a good portion of his day to animals. Nothing said he had to give up investigating, but he would need to cut back on his work load. It was something he planned to do in the future, but really, what he was waiting for?

After completing their tour, they thanked Bob and Joan for their hospitality.

"Think you'd be open to me driving that thing home?" Clay asked.

"You want to drive a Mini?" Abby laughed. "The same man who claimed he wouldn't fit wants to drive it?"

"Yeah." Clay grabbed her around the waist and pulled her against his chest. Lowering his mouth to hers, he watched her eyes flutter closed, anticipating a kiss. "Give me the keys," he whispered against her lips.

Abby's eyes flew open and she attempted to twist away from him. "That was mean."

"Stop." Clay laughed as Abby tried to escape. "Play nice or else Bob and Joan will call the police on us."

Abby stilled. "Fine, here." Thrusting the keys into his hand, she reluctantly resigned herself to the passenger seat.

"What kind of key is this?" Clay held up a circular disk. He opened the door and slid the seat all the way back before climbing in beside her. Finding a slot in the dashboard, Clay inserted the disk and pressed the start button. "My truck's so old it has an actual key on the column."

"We need to get you a more up-to-date vehicle," Abby

said, giggling. "I can totally see you working undercover in a bright yellow Mini Cooper."

"Oh, yeah, I would completely blend in with my surroundings then." Clay laughed. "How about we stop and grab a bite on the way home? There's an amazing barbecue place on the outskirts of town."

"I bet Texas barbecue can't compare to South Carolina barbecue." Abby glanced at him, the corners of her mouth curling upward. "Just kidding. I know there's no beating Texas."

"There sure isn't." Clay's grip on the steering wheel tightened as they rode in silence for a few long moments. Normally, he enjoyed the quiet, but his closeness to Abby in her car made it all but impossible for his arm not to touch hers. Coupled with the glimmer of hope that they might have a future together, it sent his libido soaring in directions he'd forgotten existed.

He fought the urge to take her hand for fear she'd sense his anxiety. Allowing her to share in his dreams was personal, borderline romantic and perfect. And perfect was out of the question, especially since she'd know the truth about her adoption and sister in less than twenty-four hours. Everything he loved about today could be gone tomorrow. Even if it wasn't, he still had to find the courage to tell her about Ana Rosa and Paulo. How would he ever find the words to tell Abby he was responsible for their deaths?

"I had an amazing time." The lilt in Abby's voice broke the silence. "Especially when I hugged that little white one. Are you ready for your own little *cria?*"

Clay exhaled a breath. "Their initial cost is much higher than sheep, but the environmental impact is less. I wouldn't have to worry about them damaging the land since they don't pull everything up by the roots when grazing. Plus, I wouldn't have to worry about hoof trimming since they don't have any. I have enough of that going on right now with the goats." He tapped the steering wheel. "Honestly, with the rate they're multiplying, the vet bills alone will bankrupt me. I'm willing to help out my clients, but it's getting to the point I'm sacrificing what I want for too many other people."

His words had come out harder than he'd intended, and he hoped Abby didn't notice his tension. Shifting slightly, he removed his phone from his pocket and checked to see if he'd missed a call from Ruby. Not seeing her number, Clay silently cursed. He'd finally allowed his heart to open again and outside circumstances were close to destroying it.

"Couldn't you sell them to one of those goat grazing operations? It's eco-friendly weed control and you'd have peace of mind they weren't sold for meat."

"That's an idea." Why hadn't he thought of that?

Out of the corner of his eye, Clay saw Abby glance at her watch. "Do you think we could get dinner to go? I forgot I have to pick up Duffy before six."

It was quarter to five. They'd make it to Ramblewood with a handful of minutes to spare.

"I'll tell you what," he said. "We'll pick up Duffy together, then you can drop me off and I'll pick us up some dinner. You two can come over to eat. That is, if you want to."

"Sure."

Abby's phone rang inside her bag.

"Excuse me a moment." She glanced at the screen. "Hello?"

Clay faintly heard a male voice on the other end of the call. Unable to make out the words, it sounded like the teacher in the Peanuts cartoon.

"Oh, my—that's wonderful!" Abby shouted. "I'm sorry, please continue."

He glanced at her. Her hand and phone partially covered her face, but there was no mistaking her giant smile.

"Yes, thank you," she said. "I look forward to discussing it with you further…you, too…goodbye."

She disconnected the call, shrieked and stomped the floorboard rapidly with her feet. "They approved the animal-assisted therapy program at the hospital! I can't believe it."

"W-wow. That's wonderful, Abby." Clay dug for the courage to congratulate her. "I'm proud of you. It's your dream job."

"Yeah, it is." Abby flopped against the seat. "At least, it was until I came here and saw Dance of Hope."

"What are you saying?" Clay swore his heart skipped a beat.

"It's something to think about and discuss further when I get home to Charleston…" Abby trailed off. "I need to really weigh the pros and cons. I'm not going to decide in five seconds one way or the other."

"How did you leave it with the hospital?" Clay hated to ask since he hadn't heard anything negative from her during the conversation.

"Well, I'm still employed by the hospital, so there's an assumption I would accept."

Clay's nerves shifted into high gear. He knew he should let her go and live her dreams, but he couldn't help think she'd fulfill them and more in Ramblewood. With him. He desperately wanted to change her mind. He was scared. Genuinely scared of losing Abby. And now the opposing team had raised the stakes. If he wanted Abby to stay, he'd need to show her how he felt, and he had only tonight to do it.

Chapter Ten

Abby ran up the stairs of the inn as quietly and quickly as humanly possible. It wasn't as if she was hiding from anyone. Okay, that wasn't entirely true. She was about to pack an overnight bag and didn't want anyone to see her sneak it out of the house. That just screamed, *Hey, I'm planning on getting some tonight.*

Duffy jumped on the bed and wagged his tail at her. "You look so cute in your new haircut, sweetie." Abby quickly fixed him a bowl of food and set it in the raised food stand. "How do you feel about a possible sleepover tonight? You like Clay, don't you?"

Who was she kidding? Duffy liked everyone. Except the UPS man. Her dog always growled when he arrived, and he was the only person who brought him puppy goodies.

After quickly stripping off her clothes, Abby jumped into the shower. The last thing she wanted was for Clay to kiss her and have his thoughts wander to an alpaca because that's what she smelled like. Duffy had gone wild at her scent.

Freshly bathed, shaved and deodorized, Abby pulled a collapsible bag from her suitcase.

"I knew this thing would come in handy." Of course,

she'd thought she would fill it with items purchased on her trip, not a change of clothes and a toothbrush.

Abby slipped on the lacy bra and panties set she'd purchased at Margarita's, a pair of fitted black yoga pants and a curve-hugging flannel shirt. Sliding her feet into sneakers, she clipped a leash on Duffy and made her descent down the stairs.

She had almost made it to the front door when she heard voices from upstairs. She broke into a run, grateful as she stumbled onto the porch without having seen anyone.

"Going somewhere?" Mazie's voice boomed from behind an urn of flowers.

"Oh, my God!" Abby dropped her bag and flattened against the wall. Duffy barked. "You scared the daylights out of me."

"I see that," Mazie snickered.

Glancing at the bag between them, Abby knew Mazie had put the pieces together. She hated having to explain herself, but Abby felt obligated since she was staying under Mazie's roof. True, it was a hotel of sorts and she owed no one anything. But Mazie was different. They'd become friends over the past week, and if Abby wasn't coming home tonight, then Mazie deserved to know. Mazie seemed the type to sit up waiting and worrying until her friends made it home safely.

"I don't know if I'm going to be back tonight." Abby wrapped and unwrapped Duffy's leash around her hand.

"Just make sure you're prepared," Mazie said.

The implication clear, Abby nodded. "I'm always prepared."

The words flew out before Abby had weighed their meaning. She wasn't prepared at all. The hospital board she'd battled for the past few years had finally granted her the opportunity of a lifetime. She'd be an integral part of designing an animal-assisted therapy program from the ground up, further increasing a patient's chance for a successful recovery.

She should be celebrating. Popping champagne corks, calling her family and friends. So why did she feel hollow? Why was her heart ready to burst? She had everything she wanted. Didn't she?

"Abby, is anything wrong?" Mazie interrupted her thoughts.

"No." She met her friend's concerned face. "Everything's perfect." Abby finally realized what it was she had wanted all along.

CLAY FLEW IN the back door of his house after he picked up dinner. He assessed the state of his home, starting with the kitchen. He grabbed all of his files, stacking them neatly on one end of the counter and shoved his laptop in its case before setting it in the dining room against the wall.

The dining room. Nothing would make the room look any better than what it was…a storage unit of sorts. He pushed what boxes were in the traffic footpath back a bit, so Abby and Duffy could easily walk past without killing themselves. Then he remembered Abby saying Clue was her favorite board game.

"Where is that box?" Clay climbed over a mountain of crap to reach the board games his sister Hannah had brought from the house. Clue was the second from the top. When he grabbed it his foot slipped, almost sending him crashing to the floor. "I really need to start going through this mess."

After vowing to himself to tackle the room in the near future, he moved on to the living room. It didn't contain much furniture—a couch, two recliners and a coffee table. A flat-screen TV hung on the wall above the fireplace, but Clay rarely turned it on.

Not remembering the last time he dusted, he pulled the pillows off the couch and gave them a good shake out on the front porch. He ran damp paper towels over every surface then pulled his emergency candles from under the sink and placed them on the fireplace mantel.

He cringed when he read the labels on the jars…sugar cookie, blueberry scones and vanilla cupcake. The candles had been Hannah's idea of a housewarming gift. She'd been a teenager back then. She was currently a sophomore in college. Her life had been constantly changing and growing, while Clay's had remained the same since the day he moved in. Until Abby had walked into his life on four-inch heels.

Clay'd had an entirely different impression of the woman during their first meeting. She had been confident, but also lost, especially compared to the strong, independent, risk-taking woman he saw now. The thing of it was, Abby probably *hadn't* changed. She was every bit as strong and independent before he met her. Hell, she had taken a huge risk driving alone in that tiny car, to a strange town, with only a note to guide her.

Clay needed to call Ruby. She'd pushed the limits of his good graces. Tomorrow was day two, and it had been long enough. If she was looking for the perfect time, he hated to break it to her, but there wasn't one.

Bounding upstairs, Clay quickly stripped the sheets off the bed and threw on a fresh set, courtesy of his mother. She was always giving him a new set of sheets for some unknown reason. He didn't have anyone to impress with his bedroom. It was stark and practical, and Clay was grateful the last few sets of sheets his mother had given him were solid colors. He didn't have the heart to tell her he had donated the floral sets to Goodwill. Why did he need so many sheets anyway? He washed them once a week and it wasn't as if he wore out the old sheets. Hell, he hadn't shared a bed with anyone since Ana Rosa.

For years, Clay had thought he'd never be able to make love to another woman. Tonight the possibility had a good chance of becoming a reality. His breath caught. Was he ready for this?

Clay glanced at himself in the bathroom mirror. Here he was, starting another relationship based on a lie. At least this time Abby knew what his profession was. The headlights of her car reflected in the upstairs windows. He brushed his teeth, rinsed and spat before running downstairs. He reached the door just as she lifted her hand to knock.

Abby had changed clothes since she dropped him off. She wore black fitted pants and a feminine pink plaid flannel shirt, which she had unbuttoned to the cleavage line, sending Clay's desire into overdrive. Not many women could make flannel sexy, but Abby had no problems in that department.

He swallowed. "Long time, no see. You look great, by the way." He bent down to kiss her on the mouth. What was supposed to be an innocent peck ran into overtime until he felt little feet pawing against his jeans. He reluctantly broke the kiss and crouched down to the floor. "Hello to you, too, Duffman."

"You tidied up, I see." Abby glanced around the kitchen. "You didn't have to do that on my account. I know you work out of your kitchen."

Clay grabbed the bag of Chinese food from the counter and led Abby by the hand into the living room.

"Clue!" She knelt in front of the coffee table. "Where did you get this?"

"I forgot my sister had brought over a whole bunch of board games before she went away to college." Clay knelt beside her and unpacked their dinner. "Are you up for the challenge?"

"Bring it." Abby helped him open the containers. "What the heck is that?"

Clay held up the lumpy bag. "Twenty fortune cookies. I hope you're hungry."

"You bet." She tore the wrapper from a set of chopsticks and dug into her lo mein noodles. He watched her carefully look around the room, wondering if she was disgusted with what she saw.

"I can see it," Abby said, nodding.

"Dust?" Clay sighed. "I tried to get it all before you got here."

"No." She waved him away. "A houseful of kids. I can see it in this house."

So could Clay...with Abby.

"PROFESSOR PLUM IN the conservatory with the lead pipe."

Clay threw the black answer envelope on the game board. "How did you solve that one so fast?"

"What does that make...seven in a row or is it eight?" Abby danced around the living room. "I beat the P.I."

As she twirled past him, Clay grabbed her wrist and pulled her onto his lap. Brushing the hair from her face, he trailed the backs of his fingers down her neck and across her chest, barely skimming the top of her breasts.

"You make me feel whole again." His statement would lead to questions, but tonight he was prepared to answer them.

"What happened to you?" Abby rested her hand over his heart.

He took a deep breath to steady his resolve. "A little

over three years ago, I was working undercover for the ATF trying to bust a gunrunning operation along the Mexican border. Part of my cover was to be a member of a biker gang who owned a motorcycle garage on the outskirts of the town where the guns were coming into the country."

Clay glanced down at Abby. Her expression was calm, serious. She nodded for him to continue. "The operation was huge and the DEA joined forces in our sting due to the high amounts of cocaine crossing the border with the guns."

"It sounds dangerous."

"Almost every investigation the ATF is involved in is dangerous." Clay shifted Abby slightly on his lap. "It went along with the job. The people we were trying to take down this time were extremely volatile. We're talking millions of dollars in guns and drugs. The extent of this raid would affect traffickers across the United States and Mexico."

Clay stared into the darkened dining room, remembering what he so desperately tried to forget.

Abby slid off his lap and sat beside him, taking his hand in hers. "We don't have to do this if you don't want to."

"It's time." He steeled himself to speak the words he had never told another living soul, not even the counselors he had been forced to see when his mission had ended. "We were there for a little over four months. During that time I met a woman named Ana Rosa and her six-year-old son, Paulo. She barely spoke a word of English, but her son had learned it in school and did most of the translating for her. My limited Spanish got me through our initial conversations and eventually we began to teach each other new words."

Duffy climbed onto his lap and lay across his legs. Clay ran his hand over the dog's back.

"Ana Rosa didn't know I was an ATF agent. She also never knew my real name. She took me at face value, assuming I was a gang member, never thinking any less of me for it. The lifestyle wasn't unfamiliar to her. Her brother, Raul, was one of the key people we were trying to take down. As time went on, Ana Rosa and I grew closer." He swallowed. "And I proposed."

Abby gasped quietly. He kept going.

"Once the investigation was over, I planned to bring Ana Rosa and Paulo back to Houston with me, which is where I lived at the time. I'd convinced myself that once she heard who I really was, she'd still want to marry me. We had too many plans for her not to. And I loved Paulo as if he were my own. Only we never had the chance."

Clay released Abby's hand and stood, needing a little liquid courage to help him through what he was about to reveal. "Care for a beer?"

Abby nodded. "Please."

He returned from the kitchen and handed her a long-neck bottle. Unable to read the expression on Abby's face, he sat beside her and continued.

"We had arranged for a major buy to go down between Raul and one of our agents. I wanted to warn Ana Rosa to stay away from the house that night because I knew the likelihood of the situation turning violent was extremely high. I also knew if I said anything to Ana Rosa, out of loyalty to her brother, she would tip him off. Instead, I bribed the manager at the restaurant where she worked to keep her on for a double shift that night. I would've been successful if Paulo's babysitter hadn't gotten sick, forcing Ana Rosa to leave early."

Clay tugged on his beer and continued to scratch

Duffy behind the neck. "She pulled up to Raul's house right in the middle of the deal. I tried to get her attention from where I was hiding outside, but instead one of her brother's guards spotted me. Hearing the commotion outside, Raul stormed out and realized he'd been set up. He grabbed Ana Rosa and Paulo and dragged them into the house, holding them hostage until we let him go. I put down my weapon in good faith. And that was when Raul gave the order to kill me. Gunfire broke out on both sides, and I watched the woman and child I loved gunned down by one of her brother's own men." He swiped at the moisture in his eyes. "They branded her a traitor because of her involvement with me. I had purposely not told Ana Rosa anything to protect her and Paulo. In the end, that's what cost them their lives."

Abby knelt beside him and clasped his face between her hands. Tears pooled in her eyes, one blink away from spilling over.

"None of this was your fault." She braced her forehead against his. "You can't keep blaming yourself for something out of your control."

"If I had thought about the babysitter. Made sure there was a backup in place. Or arranged for her to take Paulo to work. I knew to cover all my bases and I didn't."

"Clay." Abby sat on the coffee table across from him. "Look at me. You can play the *what if* game for the rest of your life, but it won't bring Ana Rosa and Paulo back. You need to accept that what happened was not your fault. No matter how good an agent you were, no one can predict with a hundred percent certainty how someone else will react in any given situation."

Clay choked back the sob threatening to tear from his throat. He hadn't let himself cry for the woman he had loved and the boy he'd planned to make his son. If he started now, he wasn't sure he'd be able to stop. Abby slipped beside him and cradled his head against her chest. The sound of her heartbeat and the feel of her hand in his hair comforted him. Duffy sat at his feet, pressing heavily against his calf, offering his own brand of comfort to Clay.

"I'm sorry." He straightened. "I know I should have told you sooner."

"Is that the first time you told anyone?"

Clay nodded. "My superiors didn't even know my full involvement with Ana Rosa."

"I'm honored you felt comfortable enough to tell me."

"It's more than that." Clay rose before Abby. "I knew our relationship couldn't go any further without my explaining why I reacted the way I have to you. When I walked away after our kiss on stage at Slater's, it had nothing to do with you and everything to do with guilt."

"You felt like you were betraying her, didn't you?"

Clay nodded. "I'm now realizing it's possible to have feelings for someone else. I haven't been with anyone since Ana Rosa. I'd like to change that. With you."

ABBY COULDN'T IMAGINE the anguish Clay had endured while watching the woman and child he loved be killed before his eyes. Tonight he had bared his soul to her and she wanted nothing more than to ease his pain.

Abby led Clay toward the staircase, turning to face him when she was two steps above him. Almost at eye level, she lightly gripped his shirt and tugged him toward her.

"Are you sure about this?" she asked.

"I've never been surer of anything."

Clay's gaze dropped from her eyes to her shoulders and then to her breasts. Peeling away her shirt, she let it fall from her fingertips to the floor. Clay's eyes became half lidded as he watched her unclasp the front of her bra, releasing her breasts. Her nipples hardened at his bold perusal. The center of her ached for his touch.

Clay made no move to touch her. He silently waited for Abby to continue. Feeling as if she were on a pedestal due to her place on the staircase, she slowly slid her yoga pants past her hips, easing them to her thighs, down to her feet and then kicking them away. Clay's eyes sparked and she reveled in his obvious approval. Standing before him in only the slightest bit of lace, Abby reached for his hands and placed them on her breasts.

He gently squeezed them, his thumbs seeking out her nipples.

"Is this what you want, Abby?" Clay growled.

"Yes." She tilted her head back thrusting her chest closer to him. She'd never been so brazen with a man before.

Clay lowered his head, his tongue tasting and teasing the taut buds. Bracing her hands on his shoulders, Abby pressed the full length of her body against his.

"You have on entirely too many clothes," she said in a husky voice that sounded foreign to her.

"So do you." Clay smiled lazily, leaving enough space between their bodies to glance down at the thin slip of lace separating her from his smoldering gaze.

"If you want them off, you have to take them off," she teased.

"Your wish is my command."

Clay began kissing her neck, trailing his lips between her breasts before his tongue seared a path down her ribs, stopping at the thin lace. Gripping her panties with his teeth, Clay gently pulled them lower.

Abby had never been more exposed to a man. The

excitement of the moment and anticipation of what was to come pooled at her center. Clay eased the lace from around her ankles and stood back to admire her.

"Stunning," he whispered. He removed his shirt, the corded muscles in his chest flexing as he undid the top button of his jeans. He lowered them to the floor until he was wearing only a pair of extremely form-fitting hunter-green boxer briefs. His arousal strained against the thin cotton, begging to be released.

"Need some help with that?" Abby's eyes shamelessly raked over his hardness.

"Please."

She slid one hand down his muscled stomach, crossing over to that perfect male V that made women stupid, before dipping her hand beneath his waistband to what could only be defined as pure magnificence.

Clay's mouth covered hers hungrily as she wrapped her fingers around him. His lips were hard, his tongue searching. Abby wound her hands around his neck, while he grabbed her backside and lifted her into the air. Instinctively, she wrapped her legs around his waist.

"I can't wait a moment longer," Clay croaked. Turning, he began to carry her up the stairs.

Abby put her hand against the wall to stop him. "No, here. Make love to me right here, right now."

ABBY STRETCHED BESIDE him in bed a few hours later.

"I need a shower. Care to join me?" She playfully rubbed her leg against his.

"I'd love to, but I don't know how clean you're going to get," Clay said, his gaze falling over her bare breasts.

"Do you plan on making me dirty?"

"Oh, I think you're dirty enough for the both of us." Clay grabbed Abby as she attempted to leave the bed.

He pulled her across his chest. "How about we skip the shower and go straight to the naked part?" Clay shifted her until she sat astride him, completely nude. Her hair fell over her shoulders, barely covering her breasts. "I've never seen a more gorgeous sight."

"Clay, don't." Abby blushed, the color spreading down her neck and across her chest.

"Don't what—tell you how I feel? I've kept too much inside for too long. I feel closer to you right now than I've ever felt to anyone."

Abby leaned down and kissed him before he could say the three words he had been aching to tell her all night. "I've never felt this close to anyone, either," she whispered against his mouth as her hips lightly rocked against him.

Clay groaned, thrusting himself deep within her once again, seeking the release they both craved until she collapsed into his arms.

Hours later, just before sunrise, Clay rolled onto his side to admire Abby asleep beside him. Beautiful, intelligent, compassionate. He watched her eyes flutter open. Smiling seductively, Abby reached to him for a kiss.

"The sun's about to come up and I need to feed the animals," Clay whispered into her hair as she ran her fingers down his chest.

"Mmm, okay. But before you go would you mind grabbing my bag from the car?"

"Bag?" Clay tilted Abby's chin up. "Did you plan on seducing me last night?"

She smiled sweetly. "A good girl always comes prepared."

"Oh, you were definitely a good girl. And a bad girl. It all depended on what hour it was." Clay lazily rolled her nipple between his thumb and forefinger. "I'll take

Duffy for a quick walk while I'm out there, too. I'm sure the little guy has his legs crossed."

"Thank you." Abby withdrew from his arms and shamelessly strolled naked from the bed to the bathroom. "I'm going to take that shower I started hours ago."

Clay was almost tempted to join her, but he had a job to do. Duffy sat beside him, wagging his tail. "Make it two jobs. Come on, little guy. Time for you to go out."

After taking Duffy for a quick walk and retrieving Abby's bag from her car, Clay squeezed back through the narrow path of boxes in the dining room. He caught his shoulder on one of them and it tumbled onto the floor.

Bending down, he set the box upright.

"Oh, no."

A framed photo of Ana Rosa and Paulo sat on the floor, the glass shattered.

Clay dropped to his knees, guilt ripping up his insides. Not just from the photo, but for sleeping with Abby. He hadn't thought of Ana Rosa once since Abby and he had started to make love. It was as if she had never existed, until now. It was a harsh reminder of what he lost.

"I am so sorry, Ana."

Clay cleaned up the broken shards of glass and returned the photo to the box, making sure he tucked it far in the back. Upstairs, he left Abby's bag on the bathroom floor.

"I have to get going after I feed the animals," Clay said from the doorway.

Abby poked her head out from behind the shower curtain. "Did you say something?"

"I have to leave. Something came up with a case."

"My case?"

Great, one more thing for him to feel guilty about. Not

only had everyone in Abby's life lied to her, he'd slept with her *and* lied to her.

"No, but I'm going to be gone for a while."

"Are you okay?" Abby ducked back behind the curtain and shut off the water. Grabbing a towel from the rack, she wrapped herself in it before stepping from the tub. "Clay, please don't pull away from me. Not now."

She reached out to touch him, but he flinched.

"That was unexpected." She grabbed a pair of jeans from her bag and tugged them on, skipping the customary underwear. Turning her back to him, she dropped her towel and pulled a tank top over her head. Abby pushed her way past him. "Duffy, it's time for us to go."

He didn't follow her down the stairs. But he wanted to. It was better this way. Let her be mad at him. It would be easier when the truth came out. Watching her tear out of his driveway, Clay marched to his dresser and grabbed his cell phone. He dialed Ruby's number, surprised when she answered the phone.

"Clay, I know what you're going to say—"

"Save it, Ruby," he snapped. "You're telling Abby and Bridgett today or I am."

"I need a little more time," she pleaded.

"You've had almost twenty-eight years of time. Abby and Bridgett deserve the truth, and every day I continue to lie to Abby for you, I'm hurting her further. Do you really want that? Ruby, I'm begging you, this needs to happen today."

"Fine. I'll call you back and let you know when and where."

Clay slammed his phone down on the dresser, amazed it didn't split in half. He needed to clear his head, and there was only one way he knew to do that.

Minutes later, he was in the barn saddling Dream

Catcher. He swung his leg up and over the saddle and slid his feet into the stirrups. With two clicks of his tongue and a squeeze of his thighs, he led Dream Catcher down one of the trails behind his house. His ranch may be small compared to the Langtrys', but it had enough acreage to provide a respectable ride.

His phone rang on the way out of the barn.

"Tonight at the salon. Six o'clock. Can you call Abby?"

"Yes, I'll call her." He hung up. Abby's world was about to be shattered.

Chapter Eleven

"Why do you want to meet me at the Curl Up & Dye?" Abby argued. "It was bad enough you wanted me out of your house this morning, now you want to meet me at a salon? They are not even open that late."

"Abby, I never asked you to leave. That was your decision," Clay pleaded begged through the phone. "Promise me you'll be there."

"Fine." Abby gripped the steering wheel. "I'll be there."

She tossed her phone across the seat of the car. It bounced, landing on the floorboard. Pulling off to the side of the road, Abby yanked a bra from her bag and quickly threw it on under her tank top. She'd driven around aimlessly for the past few hours not wanting to face Mazie. She ran a brush through her hair and applied mascara and lip gloss. Looking a bit more presentable, she headed for the Bridle Dance ranch.

"What a pleasant surprise," Kay said as Abby emerged from the Dance of Hope building and into the hippotherapy corral area.

"I hope you don't mind, but I put Duffy in your yard with Barney."

"Not at all." Kay tilted her head. "Is everything all right?"

"Everything is hunky-dory."

"Just know I'm available if you ever want to talk about it," Kay said. "And since you're here, I am down an assistant today, so if you wouldn't mind pitching in and helping out with a cognitive therapy session, I'd really appreciate it."

"I'd love to." Abby was not only honored, she was thrilled to work and take her mind off Clay. "What do you need me to do?"

"You'll be working with Darcy, one of our therapists. Cognitive therapy on a horse is very similar to cognitive therapy off a horse. We have an entire course that the patient rides through with individual stations containing a different task for them to complete." She pointed to a corner of the corral. "The first station involves riding up to the mailbox, opening it, removing the mail, closing it, reopening it, putting the mail back inside, closing it and putting the flag up. Then they move onto another station where they'll grab a series of flags from a couple of poles and then reattach the flags to another set of poles a few feet away. Our course has ten stations, and we tailor it to each individual. We also swap out the stations on a regular basis so the patients won't get bored with the same therapy over and over again. This involves a higher level of motor-skill planning to execute each task. I'm sure all of this is very familiar to you."

Abby followed Kay past the corrals to a path that wound through the shaded oak trees. After a round of introductions, Abby met a seven-year-old boy with Down syndrome.

"Bobby's a pro at this course, aren't you?" Darcy rubbed the boy's back. "Bobby, we have somebody new working with us today. This is Abby."

Abby walked to the boy's side and held out her hand to him. He eagerly shook it, not wanting to let go.

Darcy laughed. "Bobby can be a bit enthusiastic at times." Leading the horse toward the first station, Bobby still kept a firm grip on Abby's hand. "You need to let go of Abby in order to get the mail."

"I want the mail," Bobby said, releasing Abby.

An hour later, they had completed the entire course. The sense of accomplishment she felt for Bobby had her fighting to keep her tears in check. Clapping enthusiastically, she rubbed Bobby's back. "Darcy was right. You are a pro."

The boy lifted his hands in the air and grinned. "I'm a champion."

"That you are." Abby looked around. Various riders were performing all sorts of hippotherapy. She knew from Kay that quite a few of them were long-term patients and would probably be here for a while. It wasn't that much different from her long-term care patients at the hospital.

Abby's chest physically ached at the thought of leaving her patients behind in Charleston. She knew whomever they hired to replace her would be just as good, if not better, than she was. Each interaction with the Dance of Hope patients brought her one step closer to a decision. When she thought about Clay's reaction to her this morning, a part of her understood it had been based on guilt. They could work through it. It still hurt, but the sting of it lessened. Without consciously realizing it, Abby made the decision to stay in Ramblewood.

Abby spent the remainder of the day working at Dance of Hope until it was almost time to meet Clay at the salon. She dropped off Duffy at the Bed & Biscuit. Her timing was perfect—Mazie was too involved in preparing dinner to pay Abby any attention. She managed to clean up, change clothes and head out without answering a single question.

When she arrived at the salon, Abby was surprised to find the lights on and Ruby waiting with Clay inside. Bridgett appeared seconds later, walking in through the back door.

"What's all this about?" Bridgett asked.

"That's what I want to know," Abby said. "Clay, what's going on?"

"There's something I need to tell the two of you," Ruby began. "This isn't easy for me, so please bear with me."

Abby and Bridgett looked at one another then back to Ruby.

"Ruby." Clay offered his arm for support.

"Oh, my God." Abby's hand flew to her chest. "This has to do with my sister, doesn't it?"

Clay maintained eye contact with Abby. "Yes."

She shook her head. "I don't understand. What do you, Ruby and Bridgett have to do with it?"

The room became deafeningly quiet. Abby heard each breath she took, every beat of her heart. "Somebody say something. Please."

"Mother?" Bridgett, eyes wide, stared at Ruby.

"You two are sisters," the woman whispered.

Abby inhaled sharply at the words. "Come again?"

"Bridgett is the sister you've been looking for," Clay confirmed, his eyes shifting between her and Bridgett.

"For real? Mom?" Bridgett's tone filled with disgust. "You had an affair with Abby's father? How could you?"

Searching Clay's face for answers, Abby stepped back. There was more. Something they hadn't said yet. "Is that what happened? You had an affair with my father?"

"No, honey." Eyeliner and mascara stained Ruby's cheeks. "I didn't have an affair with Walter."

Abby heard the words, but the pieces weren't fitting together. "So then you hooked up after my parents split?" She looked at Bridgett. "It's the only possible way you could be my sister. H-how old are you?"

"I'll be twenty-eight on the thirteenth," Bridgett answered, confusion etched across her features.

Abby reached for the chair behind her. "The thirteenth of what?"

"October." Bridgett shrugged. "Why? I don't understand what's going on."

"How can this be?" Abby stared at Clay for an explanation.

"Abby, you need to sit down." He approached the two women. "Bridgett, so do you."

"Would somebody please tell me what the hell is going on?" Bridgett demanded. "And don't tell me to sit down."

"Bridgett," Abby said. "You and I are twins. We have the same birthday." Her voice shook. "I don't understand." She turned to Ruby. "If you didn't have an affair with Walter, and you're Bridgett's mother and Maeve is my mother then how is any of this possible?"

"Am I adopted?" Bridgett fell backwards into a stylist's chair. "M-Mom, please tell me the truth."

"You're not adopted." Ruby crossed the room to Abby. "Abby—"

"No, no, no." She shook her head and laughed. "Don't even go there. I know who my mother is. You can't possibly be—"

Abby looked past Ruby, through the front windows of the salon. Outside, people and cars went by, not a care in the world. She wanted to be one of them. This—this was a joke. A cruel, cruel joke and she wasn't going to listen to any more of it.

"I have to get out of here." Abby ran for the door. Stopping when she heard Ruby's voice.

"The adoption agency told me you were going to a young couple. Your parents."

"No, you must be mistaken." Abby thought back through all her parents' photo albums. She had wondered why there weren't any photos of her mother pregnant with Abby. Maeve had explained they were lost during a move and then quickly changed the subject. She had received the same quick dismissal when she attempted to discuss Walter's note telling her to find her sister. "Oh, my God. It's true."

Ruby wrung her hands. "I never for one second thought your parents wouldn't tell you that you were adopted."

"Mom!" Bridgett yelled. "I have a twin sister and you never told me? How could you give her away?"

"You gave me away." The realization of Bridgett's words gripped her lungs and squeezed tightly. Abby lowered herself into one of the waiting area chairs. "What did you do, play eenie-meenie-miney-mo?"

"It wasn't like that," Ruby said. "I didn't know I was pregnant with twins."

Bridgett's eyes narrowed. "How could you not know, Mother?"

"The doctor didn't even know. One baby was on top of the other, and he heard only one heartbeat. I couldn't afford an ultrasound. I didn't have any money or a job. I was recently divorced from one man, pregnant by another. Your grandparents didn't want anything to do with me. I came to Ramblewood with nothing, and I thank God every day that Fran and Ed Carter took me in."

"Hello?" Abby waved her hands. "If you didn't have an affair with my father, then who is my father?"

"Some guy in the Air Force that didn't even know Mom was pregnant before he was transferred off overseas." Bridgett sighed.

"You never met your father?" Abby asked.

"I've never met anyone in my family outside of my mom and well…you."

"I'm sorry, what? Where are your grandparents?" Abby couldn't believe Bridgett didn't have a single family member other than Ruby.

"When Mom got pregnant, they disowned her. She was a military brat herself, and after a while she lost track of where they were."

"That doesn't make any sense. If I can find my sister, you can find your grandparents, especially with the aid of a private investigator."

"I never had the need to." Bridgett hugged herself. "If they didn't want to be a part of my life, I didn't want them in mine."

"So my father is some random soldier and Walter wasn't even biologically related to me?" No wonder it was so easy for him to walk away when he and Maeve had divorced. Abby wasn't his child.

"Ruby," Clay said. "Are you telling them the truth about their father?"

Abby suddenly remembered the picture of her father that Alfred had taken. "Darren Fox."

Ruby's eyes bugged at the mention of his name.

Abby snapped her fingers. "Walter was in town because of Darren." It all made sense now. Walter's note wasn't just about finding her sister. She had been right all along. It was a deathbed confession.

"The mayor is their father?" Clay asked Ruby.

"Darren's my what?" Bridgett stepped within inches of her mother. "My father has been in this town my entire life and you didn't tell me?"

"Darren was married when I got pregnant with you both. He wanted me to take care of things, but I couldn't do it. I refused."

"Unbelievable." Bridgett paced the length of the room. "Do you have any idea how many times I served him breakfast and lunch? And now you're telling me he's my father. That man looked me straight in the eyes a million times and never said a word. He barely ever tipped me."

"Abby." Clay stood in front of her, taking her hands in his. "I am so sorry."

"For what?" She shrugged away from him. She didn't want to be comforted. She wanted answers. "You did exactly what I paid you to do. You found my sister."

"I want to know how you could give one of us away," Bridgett ordered. "Who splits up twins?"

"I'd like to know how Walter fit into all of this," Abby said.

Ruby's fingers trembled as she wiped away her tears. "Darren and Walter were in the Air Force together. Darren had confided in Walter about my pregnancy, fearing the affair would end his marriage. When I wouldn't get rid of the baby—" she shot a glance at Abby "—your mom and dad offered to adopt you."

"Why didn't they adopt me and Bridgett if you were so eager to give me away?"

"You two were born almost half an hour apart, and when Bridgett came, I thought it was a sign I was meant to have a baby of my own. I promised to give Walter and Maeve their child and I did. A second child was never part of the bargain."

Abby couldn't listen anymore. "I wasn't a bargain.

I was a baby. Your baby." Her heart actually hurt, and she was finding it difficult to breathe. "I need to get out of here."

Out on the street, Clay caught up to her. "Where are you going? I don't think you should be alone right now."

"Clay, I don't want your sympathy or your pity. All I want is answers. If Darren isn't in town, then I want his damn phone number so I can track him down."

"Darren's back. Ruby called him this morning and he does want to talk to you."

Knowing that she'd meet her biological father for the first time terrified her. She prayed the anger from what she had just learned would conquer that fear and give her the strength she needed to face him. How sweet was it that the man who had wanted to abort her would grant her this meeting?

"Will you take me to him?" she asked.

"We can go right now."

Abby steadied her nerves. Bridgett's voice carried into the street as she berated Ruby for keeping such a secret. To find out her life was a complete lie was one thing, but for Bridgett to find out her father had been around her entire life and had never acknowledged her was unfathomable.

Clay gripped her hands. "Even though all of this pans out on paper, I am urging all of you to get a DNA test to confirm it."

"Absolutely, no doubt there." Abby squared her shoulders. "Please take me to the sperm donor."

CLAY ADMIRED ABBY'S wry sense of humor through all of this, though he assumed she did it out of self-preservation. He held his truck door open for her and she climbed in. Neither one of them spoke a word during the drive to Darren's house. When they arrived, it was painfully evident Darren had confessed his affair to his wife—a large red handprint bloomed across his face.

"Abby." Darren stood back and admired her. "You are an extremely beautiful young woman."

She laughed bitterly. "And your other daughter? What about her? You haven't acknowledged Bridgett. How do you think she'll feel when she learns that you want to be a part of my life and talk to me when you ignored her for the past twenty-eight years? Don't you care?"

"Let's not do this outside." Darren stepped into the foyer. "We'll go into my den and talk."

Clay followed Abby into the bookcase-lined room. Darren closed the French doors and motioned for them to have a seat in the burgundy leather club chairs near the fireplace. Sitting across from them, Darren leaned back in his chair.

"You probably have many questions and I will be happy to answer all of them. But I'd like to tell you my side of what happened twenty-eight years ago. I'll start off by saying I'm not proud of what I did, but once the lies started, I didn't know how to stop it."

"I'm listening." Abby spotted a decanter filled with amber liquid, rose from her chair and poured herself a glass. "I'm sure you don't mind your daughter fixing a glass of— What is this?" She lifted the glass to her nose and swirled it around. "Bourbon." She raised her glass in the air. "Hey, congrats, you're a dad."

Clay fought a smile as Abby rejoined them and gestured for Darren to continue.

"I was twenty-four when I found out Ruby was pregnant. I was married and already had a child of my own. And before you ask, you have three half siblings who do not know you exist. That will be corrected in the morning."

Clay watched Abby's expression as Darren spoke. The deep lines in her forehead had softened when Darren mentioned his other children.

The mayor leaned forward in his chair. "I'm not saying what I did was right by any means. I can tell you I was young, impetuous and really didn't think how it would affect anyone except me, at that time. I can't lie and tell you I tried to convince myself that the truth would not hurt my wife. My marriage is probably over, but that's my cross to bear." He swallowed. "I did what I did to protect my reputation and myself without giving any thought to how Ruby felt. Walter was a great friend of mine, and when I confided in him, he told me about his infertility issues. When you serve in the military with someone and they have your back on the frontline, they have your back on the home front, too. Wanting a child of his own so badly, Walter offered to adopt the baby."

Abby clicked her tongue. "That was a pretty simple arrangement. Then I would be gone from your life forever. But I don't understand how that would work out with both of you being in the service together. If my parents were trying to get on-base housing, you would've still seen me on a regular basis."

Darren shook his head. "My tour was up and I wasn't reenlisting. I knew your father would be shipped off to another base and I wouldn't see you again."

"That was convenient. But what happened when you found out there were two babies?"

"I was furious. I wanted Ruby to give your parents the other child. I begged her to, but she refused. When I threatened to tell your parents about the other baby, figuring they might have legally been able to claim her and declare Ruby an unfit mother, Ruby threatened to shoot my balls off on top of telling my wife about our affair."

"Way to go, Mom." Abby raised her glass in the air in celebration.

Clay was surprised to hear her use the word *Mom* in connection with Ruby so quickly.

"Walter did eventually find out that Bridgett existed, and he really wrestled with his conscience about keeping you two apart. He only did so because I begged him to leave it alone."

"So the moral of the story is that you were a coward and now that you've been called out on it you—what?—want a relationship with me? Want to tell me to leave you alone? What do you want?"

Darren leaned forward. "Well, that's entirely up to you. I can honestly say I've matured over the past twenty-eight years, and I have wondered about you every single day of my life. At least I got to see what was going on in Bridgett's life even if I couldn't be a part of it."

"You could've been a part of her life any time," Abby said. "You chose not to be."

"I chose not to turn her life upside down with my self-ish need to come clean."

As much as Clay hated to admit it, a part of him saw Darren's side of things. It must have been hard standing on the sidelines, watching your child take her first steps, speak her first words, go on her first date and never be able to say a word. Never offer congratulations when she brought home a great report card or when she graduated high school.

"Bridgett says you never even left her a decent tip." Abby squared her shoulders. "I don't know what I want as far as you're concerned. Much of it will depend on Bridgett. I don't want to do anything that will hurt her more because she has to live with the fact that the father she thought didn't know she existed has been watching her for all these years. That's sad *and* creepy. I don't know what to tell you, Darren, but at some point, I'd like the opportunity to meet your children, my half siblings. What are they? Boys? Girls?"

"Two boys and a girl."

"And are your parents still alive?"

"You have grandparents, too, and as soon as you leave, I will be calling them and letting them know you two exist. Whether or not you meet or have a relationship with them is up to you. I can provide you with all the information, and I will give you a complete medical history, because you do deserve to know that." He rubbed the back of his neck. "I'll say this, and I'm not judging your parents, but I had no idea you didn't know you were adopted. In the back of my mind, I always figured you were looking for me, wanting to know who your birth father was. I knew this day was coming. It simply didn't happen quite the way I expected it to."

"Fair enough. For now, I'm going to leave things as they are. I'll get your information from Clay and I will be in touch. I need some time to process this, and I need to pay my parents a visit."

Clay had known Abby would leave town eventually, but to hear her speak the words aloud made his chest constrict. Of course, she would confront her parents. She had every right to do so. He had imagined her doing it over the phone. Driving from Texas to Pennsylvania in her current condition didn't sound like such a good idea.

After saying their goodbyes, Clay drove Abby back to the Bed & Biscuit. "When are you leaving?"

"Tomorrow."

"Let me go with you," he said.

"I need to put my big-girl panties on and handle this on my own. I appreciate the offer, though. I need some time to think and reevaluate my life since it's not what I thought it was."

"Are you coming back?" Clay ran his palms over the steering wheel.

"I don't know." Abby opened the truck door. "I would like to say yes, but I can't make any promises right now. I appreciate everything you've done for me and I don't know where things go from here. I wish I could tell you more."

"Is this where we say goodbye?" Clay looked at Abby, unable to bear the thought that this was the last time he'd see her. There were no promises she'd return. Only an emptiness slowly filling his heart.

"I think it's best, instead of dragging it out tomorrow."

"I never wanted you to get hurt in any of this."

"It was inevitable." She shrugged. "Just the fact that a sister was kept from me my entire life was painful. There was no way to come out of this unscathed. I started to realize that once I got here. I even questioned if I truly wanted to find out the truth."

"Any regrets?"

Abby smiled. "No, Clay, I don't regret a single moment of my trip. Not a single one."

Clay tried to catch his breath, but his world was folding in on him.

"I need to ask you one thing before I go."

"Anything," he whispered.

"That day, when you burst into the salon and practically dragged Ruby into the back, that was the day you found out, wasn't it?"

Clay nodded, unable to speak the words.

"So when you made love to me, didn't you wonder how

I'd react to your knowing and keeping my adoption from me? That wasn't an ethics violation. You could have told me that much without revealing who my mother was."

Clay hesitated before meeting Abby's eyes. "I was afraid you'd leave."

"But, you did it anyway. You slept with me knowing this would change everything." She shook her head. "You know what? Don't answer."

Abby leaned across the seat and kissed Clay on the cheek before jumping out the door. He watched her run up the porch stairs of the Bed & Biscuit, never looking back once. The sharp ache in his chest spread through his body. It was the feeling of losing someone he loved once again. He prayed there was some hope of her returning to Ramblewood. If this was the last time they were together his heart couldn't take it. Her kiss, that final kiss, felt like goodbye. Forever.

The sound of the screen door banging against the door jamb rattled through him like a gunshot. The front door of the inn closed behind Abby, and she was gone. The night air chilled the cab of his truck. If only he had told her how he felt, maybe it would have made a difference. If only he had said the words.

"I love you, Abby."

Chapter Twelve

"I'm sorry things turned out the way they did for you." Bridgett leaned against the outside wall behind The Magpie.

"Same here," Abby said. "But I'm glad to find out you're my sister."

"Yeah." Bridgett continued to stare at her feet.

"Well, I will definitely keep in touch and let you know what's going on. And good luck if you decide to talk to Darren."

"Fat chance of that ever happening." Bridgett's eyes narrowed. "The man wanted nothing to do with me all these years. I can promise you, until his dying day, I want nothing to do with him."

"I completely understand. You have my number, so call me if you need anything, and I'll talk to you soon."

"Have a safe trip." Bridgett ducked back into The Magpie. Abby stared at the closed door. She wasn't sure what she expected from her sister. Heck, she didn't know what she expected from herself.

She slid behind the wheel of her car, then headed toward the Bridle Dance Ranch. She had said all of her goodbyes except for one. She owed Kay Langtry that much.

Abby drove down the ranch's dirt road. Red harvesters sat off to the side, waiting to gather the falling pecans.

It was harvest time and Abby would miss it. She would miss many things about Ramblewood, but the Bridle Dance Ranch and the Dance of Hope Hippotherapy Center claimed top billing. Next to Clay. She didn't dare think about him for fear she'd start crying. That was the last thing she wanted—her eyes were puffy enough already.

Abby had called Kay earlier and given her a brief rundown of last night's events. The woman waited for her on the front porch of the main house.

Kay's warm hug enveloped Abby the way a mother's hug should.

"I'm sorry to see you go," Kay said. "Promise me you'll still consider working for us despite everything else. Follow wherever your heart leads you, Abby."

"I haven't ruled anything out." She gazed out over the ranch. The morning mist still hung close to the ground, giving it an ethereal appearance. "I'm not going to make any decisions until I talk to my parents. I don't want my emotions to cloud my judgment one way or the other."

"That is a very responsible way of looking at it." Kay walked Abby to her car. "I do hope to see you again. And I speak for Barney when I say he hopes to see Duffy soon."

Abby gave Kay one last hug goodbye before climbing back into her car. Driving off the ranch, she braved a look in the rearview mirror. The pain of leaving Ramblewood behind was almost unbearable. She needed to be sure that feeling was still there in the future. She didn't trust her own decisions right now so it was best not to make any at all.

"Are you ready for another ride?" Abby tilted the rearview mirror so she could see Duffy in his doggy booster seat.

Abby blocked her phone number and dialed her parents' house. When her mother answered the phone, Abby quickly hung up. Yes, it was juvenile, but necessary. She didn't want to drive all that way to find out her parents were on another cruise.

The sun shone through Abby's sunroof, bathing her in warmth. Her body had shivered ever since she had learned Maeve and Walter weren't her biological parents. And as much as she hated to admit it, she did see a lot of Ruby in herself. Abby didn't know if she should be happy or frightened by that prospect. Darren was another story. She didn't see any of him in herself and she would definitely take Clay's advice about getting a DNA test.

Leave it to Abby to fall in love with a P.I. in the heart of Hill Country. She inwardly laughed at her own admission. No matter how she looked at it, she was in love with Clay. Now that she knew, the question remained: What was she going to do about it?

CLAY STARED AT the boxes in his dining room for hours. He replayed the night he had lost Ana Rosa and Paulo a thousand times over, comparing that horrific night to Abby's leaving. He knew they were nowhere remotely close to each other, but the pain of possibly losing Abby ranked a close second.

The clock on the wall ticked loudly in the silent house. Every hour Clay wondered if Abby had already left town. Unable to bear it any longer, he hopped in his truck and drove to the Bed & Biscuit. He sagged against the door when he turned into the parking lot and didn't see her Mini Cooper.

He drove to The Magpie, double-parked in front and ran inside. He interrupted Bridgett in the middle of taking someone's order to ask if she'd seen Abby this morning. He couldn't imagine her leaving without saying goodbye to Bridgett first. When she told him Abby had left a couple of hours earlier, Clay hoped she'd driven out to Bridle Dance. Maybe she was still there, chatting with Kay about hippotherapy. He needed to hear that Abby was coming back to accept the job after she confronted her family.

But Clay didn't see Abby's car anywhere when he drove onto the ranch. He pulled alongside the Langtrys' house, knocked once and let himself in as he'd done all his life. When he realized the house was empty, he started for the back door. Kay reached for the screen at the same time he did.

"I was looking for you." Clay's breath was ragged from running through the house.

"I gathered when I saw your truck drive in." Kay pulled a stool out from under the kitchen's butcher-block island and gestured for Clay to sit down. "Abby left here an hour ago. She headed straight for the interstate."

The remaining energy Clay had drained from his body as he collapsed onto the stool.

"Give her time." Kay sat next to him, clasped his hands and turned him to face her. "That girl's carrying a world of hurt on her shoulders right now. She needs to sort this out before she's any good to you, herself, or whatever job she decides to accept."

"Abby told you the hospital reversed their decision on the animal-assisted therapy program?"

"Yes, and I told her the Dance of Hope offer was still on the table." Kay squeezed his hands. "Abby hasn't made a decision one way or the other."

"How could she not choose Charleston?" The words stung as he spoke them aloud. "It's her dream job."

"It *was* her dream job." Kay rose from the stool, topped two tall glasses with ice from the freezer and filled them with lemonade. "Abby's life has completely changed since the day she arrived. Things that were a priority a few weeks ago, no longer hold the same weight today. She was very honest with me this morning, saying she didn't want to decide until after she spoke with her parents. She doesn't want her emotions to get in the way."

Clay sipped his lemonade. "Do you think I should go after her? It's a long way for her to drive with that much on her mind."

"What would you do if you saddled your horse to head out on a trail to clear your head and someone said you weren't capable of going alone because you had too much to think about?"

"Point taken."

"You're doing exactly what Abby said she wouldn't do. You're letting emotions make decisions for you. I don't know what happened when you were away, but you came back a changed man. Abby played a big part in drawing out the Clay we all know and love. Don't retreat into a protective shell just because she's gone. You can't live for someone else. You have to live for yourself first or you will never be any good to anyone."

Clay nodded. If Abby returned to town, he needed to show he was ready to make a commitment. Kay was right. He needed to start with himself, and that meant finally moving into his house.

"The day you gave Abby my phone number, did you send her my way because you thought I was the man to find her sister or because you thought Abby was the woman for me?"

Kay grinned. "Both. I saw a light in Abby and I thought she'd be perfect for you. I've watched you grow up, both here with my boys and on your parents' ranch. I know you well enough to recognize you were just a little lost and needed someone to help you find your way."

"Do you still feel Abby and I are meant to be together?"

"You know how when you leave a light on for too long it burns out quicker than if you turn it off and let it rest every once in a while?"

Clay laughed. "Yeah, I do. Although I'm not sure how Abby would feel being compared to a lightbulb."

"True. Let's keep that one to ourselves." Kay sipped the last of the lemonade in her glass. "You get yourself good and sorted before you see Abby again. I'm not saying you can't call her to talk or ask how she's doing. Take this time, however long it is, and use it to your advantage. Maybe Abby won't come back to Ramblewood, and then you'll have to ask yourself if you're willing to go to her."

Clay hadn't considered moving to Charleston. He could be a private investigator anywhere. He'd need to get relicensed. Maybe there was land outside of Charleston and he could still have his alpaca farm. Either way, it wasn't unobtainable and that meant Abby wasn't unobtainable. That's if she'd have him.

"Thank you." Clay placed his empty glass on the counter. "You've given me quite a bit to think about."

"You know my door is always open for you boys."

Clay gave the woman he considered his second mother a hug, then headed into town. He had a lot of work ahead of him.

ABBY DROVE THE sixteen hundred miles to her parents' house in Pennsylvania in two days, stopping for a shower and a few hours' sleep somewhere in the middle of Kentucky. By that time, her anger had faded into sorrow then back to anger again, giving her the second wind she needed to continue.

She had so many questions, and she couldn't see her mother possibly explaining her way out of this one. And then there was Steve. The stepfather she considered her father. Did he know about this the entire time? Or had her mother lied to both of them? How much did Wyatt know?

Every question felt like paranoia, and then Abby realized she had a right to question everything. She tried calling Bridgett a few times from the road, but her sister never answered. Space was probably a good thing for all of them. Abby hoped once Bridgett had a chance to cool off, she'd like to have a relationship of some sort with her.

Her life was spinning out of control. Was she starring in a soap opera? And the one person she had put all her faith in had hidden the truth from her. Regardless of the rules, why hadn't Clay told her the minute he had found out? This wasn't just a case of a long-lost relative— Abby's entire life had been a lie. Not that finding out sooner would've made anything any better. But he had purposely kept the truth from her. Their lovemaking had been based on a lie. Abby had never felt more used in her entire life. He knew she'd leave when she found out the truth. He'd said as much.

The pain in Clay's face when he told her about Ana Rosa flashed in Abby's mind. Maybe he had tried to protect her. How could someone who suffered that deeply be malicious? He couldn't be. Clay had done what he thought was right. In reality, it didn't matter if she had found out years or five minutes ago. It wouldn't have changed the facts. Abby's whole life had been a lie.

She hated that she had left Bridgett to deal with the

fallout and Darren Fox by herself. It was one thing for Abby to find out he was her father, it was completely different for Bridgett. A man she saw on a regular basis had stood by and done nothing to support her the entire time she'd been growing up. He should have paid child support, paid for schooling. New clothes.

Bridgett didn't want to be a waitress all her life. From the looks of Darren's house, the man had done very well for himself. Abby bet he had established college funds for his other children. Despite Bridgett stating school wasn't her thing, Abby knew her sister would have leaped at the opportunity to go to cooking school if it had been offered.

Of the two of them, Abby didn't know who had it worse. She could go home to Charleston and be anonymous. Bridgett didn't have that luxury. She must hate Abby for it. And she wouldn't blame Bridgett one bit. Her life had been calm and quiet before Abby had blown into town with Walter's note.

She gripped the steering wheel. "Walter, this is one gift I wish you had kept to yourself."

Abby fumbled for her phone and switched it back on. She dreaded the amount of voice mail waiting for her, but for the next few days, she didn't care.

"Hey, Mom," Abby said when her mother answered the phone. "I just wanted to make sure you and Dad are home."

"I answered the phone, didn't I?" Her mother laughed. "What are you up to, dear?"

"Oh, not much. Just driving into town to see you."

"You are?" Abby could hear her mother call for her father in the background. "Steve, Abby's on her way home. When will you get here, honey?"

The word *honey* made Abby sick to her stomach. "In

about twenty minutes. So I suggest you don't go anywhere."

"Abby, is everything all right?"

"It will be."

Disconnecting the call, Abby turned up the volume on the radio, determined to enjoy the next twenty minutes before her world tilted off its axis again.

ABBY PULLED INTO her parents' driveway and cut the car's engine. Reaching into the backseat, she unclipped Duffy from his safety harness. "Ready to rock 'n' roll?"

Duffy barked and jumped over the center console, wagging his tail anxiously. It had been quite a while since their last stop and he was ready for a potty break.

While her only loyal friend did his business, she looked at the house where she had grown up. It seemed surreal to her now. The place she called home, yet never felt she belonged. Now she knew why.

The front door opened and her mother walked out onto the front stoop. Abby inhaled sharply and braced herself for what could potentially be more lies.

With Duffy by her side, she trudged up the stairs.

"Abby." Her mother pulled her into a hug. "What a wonderful surprise. Why didn't you tell us you were coming?"

Stiffly, Abby withdrew from the embrace. She found it hard to look her mother in the eye.

"Where's Dad?" Abby asked.

"Steve," Maeve called. "Look who's here."

After being ushered through the door, Abby shortened Duffy's leash. She needed to feel his little body pressed against hers.

"You'll never guess where I've been," Abby said as her father walked into the room.

"It's good to see you, princess." Steve hugged her. His typical relaxed demeanor compared to her mother's edginess told Abby this was her mother's worst fear. How many times had Abby come home upset and Maeve had wondered for a moment if it was because Abby had discovered the truth?

"Remember when I asked you about Walter's note and you dismissed it?" Abby focused on her mother. "Well, I decided to do a little investigating. Actually, that's not entirely true. I drove to Ramblewood, Texas, and hired a private investigator. Can you guess what he discovered?"

All color drained from her mother's face.

Abby glanced at her father. "You may want to catch Mom because I think she's about to faint."

Steve looked at his wife. "Maeve? Are you okay?"

Abby waved her hand. "She'll survive. Let me fill you in on the details. Turns out Mom's been keeping a big secret."

"Abby, please," her mother begged.

"Please what?" She tried not to shout. "Please understand? Please don't say anything in front of Dad? You've got to help me out here, Mom, because you haven't exactly been forthcoming, have you?"

"What is she talking about, Maeve?" her father asked.

"Dad, I'm just going to come straight out and ask you. Did you know I was adopted?"

He furrowed his brow. "Abby, you know I adopted you."

"No, I mean a hundred percent adopted."

"Oh, dear," Maeve whispered.

"Turns out I not only have a long-lost sister that I didn't know about, she's my twin. Wait, it gets better. Mom isn't my mom. A woman named Ruby Jameson is my mother, and my father, my biological father, is a man named Darren Fox, not Walter Davidson."

"Twins?" Maeve struggled to regain her composure. "What are you talking about?"

"Mom, please stop lying."

"What is going on?" Steve demanded. "Abby, what are you talking about?"

She recounted the past week and a half to her parents in detail, in between her mother's sobs and her father's *I can't believe this*. Somehow Abby managed to relay the entire story without shedding a tear or raising her voice.

"Abby, you don't understand the situation at the time."

"You're not denying this?" Steve asked. "Maeve, how could you keep this a secret?"

"It's not that simple." Maeve's voice rose an octave. "I never knew there were two girls. Walter never told me."

"Why didn't you tell me I was adopted?" Abby asked.

"Abby, Walter and I tried to conceive for years before we found out he had an extremely low sperm count. The chances of us having a child of our own were almost nil. Walter was not only devastated, he was embarrassed, and considered himself half a man for not being able to give me a child. We didn't tell anyone we couldn't conceive. We had talked about artificial insemination, but the thought of it bothered me. When Walter told me there was a single mom looking to give up her child for adoption as soon as it was born, Walter and I didn't need to think twice."

"It still doesn't answer my question. Why didn't you tell me I was adopted?"

"Walter and I had been away from home for two years. Nobody we knew would have known if I was pregnant or not. So to save Walter's pride we told everyone I gave birth to you. When they asked why we never said anything during the pregnancy, I told them there had been so many complications I didn't know if I would be able to carry to term and I didn't want to jinx it."

"That's quite a background story you concocted, Mom."

"I'm not denying that, Abby. When your father and I separated a year later, I truly felt you were my daughter. It was no different than if I gave birth to you. Nobody knew except for Walter and me, so I didn't see any point in telling everyone. Yes, I kept it to myself, but it wasn't for malicious reasons. I had planned on telling you one day, until Wyatt was born. I don't know if you remember, but you were so upset when I told you Steve and I were expecting a baby. You wanted to know if we were going to push you out of the family since we had a baby of our own on the way. That's heartbreaking for a mother to hear." She brushed away tears. "After Wyatt was born, you still asked if we considered you part of the family. You would question your father if he loved Wyatt more than he loved you because Wyatt was biologically his. So, I decided it was best not to tell you that you weren't biologically my child, either. Abby, you felt so alienated as it was." Maeve sobbed. "I didn't want to make it any worse for you. I thought I was doing the right thing. As a mother, you'll do anything to protect your child."

"This didn't protect me, Mom," Abby said.

"Yes, baby, it did. You went through life knowing you were a part of us, of this family." She gestured to Steve. "And rightfully so. I don't love you any less than I love Wyatt. Giving birth doesn't make you a mother. Your family is who you choose to love in life and, Abby, I chose you. Wyatt happened, but I *chose* you."

Abby's entire body trembled. "That's where you're wrong. I never felt like I belonged. I always thought something was missing. I couldn't understand why I didn't look like either one of you. Not that I look anything like my sister who towers over me or my mother with her flaming red hair. But I do see a lot of myself in both of them."

She collapsed onto the couch. Between the drive and the stress, she was exhausted. "I—I need to lie down. It's been a long drive and I need to sleep for a while."

Her mother tried to help her from the couch, but Abby shied away from her touch. Her legs shut down. She had never felt weaker in her entire life. She looked at her father. Without asking, he wrapped his arm around her and guided her down the hallway. Once in the guest room, he eased her onto the bed.

"Can I get you anything? Water, aspirin, a shot of rum?" He smiled.

Leave it to her father to add a little levity to the situation. Duffy jumped onto the bed beside her and threw his body across her lap.

"I just need a nap. It was a long drive."

"Abby, for what it's worth, I truly believe your mother when she says she didn't know your sister existed. I'm not saying I agree with her decisions, but I do remember how you acted when you found out Wyatt was on the way."

"So it's all *my* fault Mom lied to me? Unbelievable."

Her father sighed. "That's not what I'm saying at all, and I think when you have a chance to calm down, take in everything your mother has said and you two talk some more, maybe you'll realize she was truly trying to protect you."

Abby sat on the edge of the bed for a long time after her father closed the door. She blew her nose for the hundredth time, waking Duffy. He looked up at her and attempted to lick her tears away.

Abby didn't want to think anymore. Her body craved sleep, and as she laid her head down and closed her eyes, visions of Clay invaded her dreams.

Chapter Thirteen

Clay tossed his truck keys onto the counter beside the office lease he had signed an hour earlier. CT Investigations officially had a location in town above Cowpokes Western Wear. He didn't know how long he'd remain an investigator once he started his alpaca ranch, but one thing was for certain, he needed a dedicated office space away from the house.

Picking up the phone, he dialed Shane's number.

"Hey, man. What are you and Lexi doing tonight?"

"Nothing," Shane said. "Did you feel like going to Slater's?"

"Not tonight. I need to ask you a favor. Remember when you offered to help me with the house?"

"I do," Shane said. "You ready to accept?"

"Yes, and I could really use some help from you and Lexi tonight."

"We'll be over shortly."

A few minutes later, Clay had a similar conversation with his parents. Once everyone had arrived, he spent the next hour recounting what happened when he was in the ATF.

Afterward, Clay's entire body felt lighter. He no longer had to keep the secret. Sometimes a story is so painful that even when you want to share it you can't, because the words alone cut through you. If it hadn't been for Abby, Clay doubted he would've been ready to tell any of it. Not surprisingly, his family and friends understood his reason for not opening up sooner.

While Lexi and his mom went grocery shopping, his father and Shane offered to open all of the boxes and look through them first to see if there was anything of Ana Rosa's in them, agreeing to set them aside for Clay to go through later. Clay didn't want any distractions from cleaning out his dining room and finally unpacking his house.

His parents left sometime around midnight, and Lexi followed shortly after, but Shane, his best friend, with a beer in hand, stayed and continued to help him through the night.

Clay stood back and admired the completely empty dining room.

"I really appreciate this." He slapped his friend on the back. "I don't know how I would've done this without you."

"We're not finished yet." Shane crossed the room and tugged the cord on the blinds. For the first time since Clay had moved in, golden light from the sunrise filtered through the window and onto the oak floor.

"This is the first time I've seen that floor," Clay said. "It's not half bad."

"With a little refinishing, it will clean up nice," Shane added. "The bones of this house are really solid."

"Eventually I'll get a dining room table."

"Eventually, my ass," Shane said. "As soon as Mayfair's opens we are driving into town and seeing what we can do to furnish this place. And don't give me any crap that you can't afford it because it's my housewarming gift three years later."

There was no sense in arguing with Shane. "Thank you. And thank your wife for that massive shopping trip she took with my mother."

"Thank her yourself," Shane said. "Now that you have food in the house, we expect to be invited over for dinner."

Clay braved a glance at the kitchen. He remembered the easy way Abby had fit into the room, even when it had been a disaster with case files everywhere.

"You miss her, don't you?"

Clay nodded, afraid if he opened his mouth he might actually say Abby's name.

He had tried calling her after he had leased his new office space and had been greeted with a *voice mail full* message. He had sent one text, but when that didn't receive a response, he'd decided to give Abby the time she needed. That and the fact that he'd called her home in Charleston and her brother had told him Abby was in Pennsylvania attempting to sort through this mess with her family.

"Have you thought about flying out to see her?" Shane asked.

"I don't even know when she'll be home."

"Doesn't she have a job to go back to?"

"I don't know anymore. She'd been leaning toward Dance of Hope when the hospital board called to say they had approved her animal-assisted therapy program. She hadn't made a decision when I last spoke to her, but after everything that happened, I can't see her still wanting to move here." It was one of the fears Clay had had from the moment he found out Ruby was Abby's mother. "Has your mother talked to her?"

"Not that I know of, but if she did, and Abby asked her to keep it quiet, she would never tell me."

Clay thought back to the day Kay had offered her a job at Dance of Hope. He tried to compare it to the day Abby received the phone call from the hospital. Her reactions weren't even comparable. She was in shock over one and had cried during the other.

He cleared his throat and met Shane's eyes. "I know this is going to sound horrible of me, but some days I wish I had kept what I found to myself."

"You say that now, but you wouldn't have been able to live with it."

"Yeah, you're probably right, but you can't deny how much easier things would be today."

"Clay, go to her. Don't let the woman of your dreams slip through your hands. It's obvious you're in love with her. So find her and tell her."

That afternoon, after Shane and Clay set his new salvaged wood trestle dining table and mismatched padded dining room chairs in place, which Lexi assured him were all the rage, he stood back and admired the view. He had to give the woman credit. The burgundy-and-brown Southwestern area rug pulled everything together the way Lexi had said it would.

Relieved to have normalcy in a room that once held so many dark memories, Clay booked a flight to Charleston. Excited to share the changes he'd made with Abby, his nerves ramped up at the thought of seeing her after the way they had left things. He didn't know how long he'd have to wait for her to come home, but he'd be there when she did.

ABBY LEFT HER PARENTS' house before sunrise and turned onto her own street well after sunset. It had been another long drive, and as much as Abby loved her Mini Cooper, she was sick to death of being in it.

Slipping her key into the lock, she opened her front door. Home. She was finally home, and it felt foreign to her.

"Abby!" Wyatt bounded down the stairs, causing Duffy to bark and spin in circles. "You're here." He gave her a body-engulfing hug. It was strange to think of her and Wyatt not sharing a single strand of DNA. He was her best friend, and though she knew he hadn't changed, their relationship felt awkward.

"I don't know what to say." Tears formed in Abby's eyes.

"Don't say anything," Wyatt said. "Nothing's changed between us. I still love you as much as I did before you left. You're still my sister regardless of who our biological parents are. None of that matters."

"I know." Abby nodded, regaining her composure. "Hey, at least the truth is out there and there are no more secrets looming over me."

"I want to hear everything about your sister and Ruby, but there's someone here who needs to see you first."

"Who?"

"Me." Clay appeared at the top of the stairs. Duffy ran up to greet him.

"How did you know I'd be getting home tonight?"

"I didn't," Clay said as he descended.

"He's been here for a few days," Wyatt said, stepping back to give them space.

"I knew you'd come home eventually. Care to take a walk with me?"

Abby stared up at the man she'd missed desperately during the past week.

"Well, since I did tell you I'd like to show you around Charleston, I guess it's only fair. Besides, after sitting for

seventeen hours, Duffy and I definitely need to stretch
our legs."

Clay gently entwined his fingers with hers. Tightening
her grip, she enjoyed the warmth of his hand. Leading
him outside, they walked toward Waterfront Park along
the Cooper River.

"How did things go with your parents?"

"My stepdad never knew any of it and my mom, well,
that was rough at first. We talked and talked until we
hashed everything out. I don't agree with her not telling me about the adoption. Especially when it comes to
medical records and hereditary problems. I don't love my
mom any less and I certainly don't hate her. I'm confused
and I have so many tainted memories now."

"Tainted how?"

"When I think back to certain events or birthdays,
they always felt off. It was as if something was missing
and I never could put my finger on what it was. Now I
understand why. It's going to take some time."

"I'd like to stand beside you while you sort through
it." Clay's voice soothed her. She'd almost forgotten how
good he sounded. He stopped walking and turned her to
face him. "I love you, Abby. I should have told you that
the night I made love to you. Hell, I should've told you
before."

"I love you, too, but I don't know if you can ever get
past what happened with Ana Rosa."

"I think if it hadn't been for you, I may not have seen
the light at the end of the tunnel. I'll never know what
would have been if I'd done things differently all those
years ago. I've lived in the past for too long. I'm ready to
move forward. You won't believe the changes I've made
to the house."

"Changes, huh?"

"I leased the office above Cowpokes, and that's the new CT Investigation headquarters so my clients no longer have to meet me in luncheonettes."

"Headquarters?" Abby grinned. "Pretty snazzy."

"I've also thought about hiring other investigators, leaving me free to run the alpaca ranch I intend to start in the near future. And I cleaned out the dining room with help from Shane, Lexi and my parents. My house is officially unpacked and I have a brand-new dining room table, compliments of Shane."

"You have been busy."

"Oh, and a houseful of food and cleaning products."

Abby laughed. "You weren't kidding when you said you'd made changes."

"I also realized none of that means anything without you by my side to share it. And I understand completely if you don't want to move to Ramblewood. I'd be willing to move to Charleston, if it means having you in my life and as my wife."

"Are you proposing?" Abby never thought she would hear Clay say he'd give up his life in Ramblewood for her. "Before you answer, what would you say if I told you I called Kay on the way home and accepted her offer?"

Clay's handsome face broke into a grin. "What about the hospital here wanting to work with you on an animal-assisted therapy program? You'd give up that opportunity?"

"It wasn't an easy decision, but after a few phone calls back and forth, the hospital agreed to hire me on as a consultant instead. I'd have to fly into Charleston once a month for a day or two."

"Fly? Abby Winchester doesn't fly."

"No, but Abby Tanner does, if it means getting home to her husband sooner."

"Is that a yes?"

"Yes!" She clapped her hands. "How does New Year's Eve sound? Because I can think of a million ways to decorate the inside of Slater's Mill. We can have this really cool barn—"

Clay stopped walking and knelt down on one knee in front of her, Duffy joining him by his side.

She grabbed his shoulders. "What are you doing? That couple over there is trying to take a picture of the Pineapple Fountain and you're in the way."

"Why don't we make this official?" Clay said as he removed a black velvet box from his pocket.

Abby's limbs almost went weak when she realized what Clay was about to do. Sure, they had just talked about it, but this…here, in front of the crowd of people that had begun to gather around them…was a dream come true. Clay opened the box, and met her gaze. "Abby Winchester, will you do me the honor of becoming my wife?"

"Yes." Abby dragged him to his feet and kissed him. "I will."

Duffy barked and the mass of onlookers applauded. Slipping the ring onto her finger, Clay grinned. "A perfect fit."

"You know, you're an excellent private investigator. Not only did you find my sister, you found me a husband, too."

"Just doing my job, ma'am." Clay dipped his head toward hers. "Just don't ever ask for a refund. You're stuck with me forever."

* * * * *

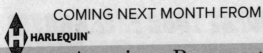
#1541 TEXAS REBELS: EGAN

Texas Rebels • by Linda Warren

Rachel Hollister feels an immediate attraction to the man who comes to her rescue after her car breaks down. What she doesn't know yet is Egan Rebel was sent to prison by a man he can't forgive—her father.

#1542 A MONTANA COWBOY

Hitting Rocks Cowboys • by Rebecca Winters

Injured jet pilot Trace Rafferty returns to Montana to sell the family ranch before resuming his military duties. But Cassie Dorney, a pregnant widow who has been caring for the ranch, just may steal his heart...and turn him back into a cowboy.

#1543 THE COWBOY'S LITTLE SURPRISE

The Hitching Post Hotel • by Barbara White Daille

Tina Sanchez can't trust Cole Slater, but she'll have to forget his betrayal and give Cole a chance to be a father—for the sake of their son.

#1544 A WIFE IN WYOMING

The Marshall Brothers • by Lynnette Kent

When big-city lawyer Ford Marshall meets hometown Wyoming girl Caroline Donnelly, he thinks they have nothing in common, except the troubled teens they're both taking care of...and the fact they are falling in love.

REQUEST YOUR FREE BOOKS!
2 FREE NOVELS PLUS 2 FREE GIFTS!

LOVE, HOME & HAPPINESS

YES! Please send me 2 FREE Harlequin® American Romance® novels and my 2 FREE gifts (gifts are worth about \$10). After receiving them, if I don't wish to receive any more books, I can return the shipping statement marked "cancel." If I don't cancel, I will receive 4 brand-new novels every month and be billed just \$4.74 per book in the U.S. or \$5.24 per book in Canada. That's a savings of at least 14% off the cover price! It's quite a bargain! Shipping and handling is just 50¢ per book in the U.S. and 75¢ per book in Canada.* I understand that accepting the 2 free books and gifts places me under no obligation to buy anything. I can always return a shipment and cancel at any time. Even if I never buy another book, the two free books and gifts are mine to keep forever.

154/354 HDN F4YN

Name	(PLEASE PRINT)	
Address		Apt. #
City	State/Prov.	Zip/Postal Code

Signature (if under 18, a parent or guardian must sign)

Mail to the Harlequin® Reader Service:
IN U.S.A.: P.O. Box 1867, Buffalo, NY 14240-1867
IN CANADA: P.O. Box 609, Fort Erie, Ontario L2A 5X3

Want to try two free books from another line?
Call 1-800-873-8635 or visit www.ReaderService.com.

* Terms and prices subject to change without notice. Prices do not include applicable taxes. Sales tax applicable in N.Y. Canadian residents will be charged applicable taxes. Offer not valid in Québec. This offer is limited to one order per household. Not valid for current subscribers to Harlequin American Romance books. All orders subject to credit approval. Credit or debit balances in a customer's account(s) may be offset by any other outstanding balance owed by or to the customer. Please allow 4 to 6 weeks for delivery. Offer available while quantities last.

Your Privacy—The Harlequin® Reader Service is committed to protecting your privacy. Our Privacy Policy is available online at www.ReaderService.com or upon request from the Harlequin Reader Service.

We make a portion of our mailing list available to reputable third parties that offer products we believe may interest you. If you prefer that we not exchange your name with third parties, or if you wish to clarify or modify your communication preferences, please visit us at www.ReaderService.com/consumerchoice or write to us at Harlequin Reader Service Preference Service, P.O. Box 9062, Buffalo, NY 14269. Include your complete name and address.

HAR13R

*Egan Rebel is the last man Rachel Hollister expects to
meet when she returns home to Horseshoe, Texas!*

*Read on for a sneak peek of
TEXAS REBELS: EGAN, the first book in*
Linda Warren's
TEXAS REBELS miniseries.

Rachel Hollister was lost.

For over an hour she'd been traveling this country
back road and the scenery had changed from mesquite
and scrub to thick woods. She'd left the blacktop some
time ago and now the road narrowed to merely a track.
She looked around for signs of human life, a barn, anything. But all she saw were woods and more woods where
the track ended.

She reached for her phone in her purse and tried to
call her brother. No signal. She looked out the window
and couldn't see power lines. Where was she? Rachel got
out of the car and an eerie feeling came over her. She
tried her phone again. Nothing. A sliver of alarm shot
through her. How was she going to get out of here? She'd
have to walk out or sit here and wait for someone to find
her. From the silence, she feared that wait might be long.
Her choices were simple. She looked down at her dress
and heels. Not ideal for walking. Her suitcase was in the
backseat, so she'd just change into jeans and sneakers,
she decided.

As Rachel moved toward the door, something caught her eye. Her heart thumped against her chest. There was a man emerging from the woods. He was hard to see because he seemed as one with his surroundings. A duster like she'd seen cowboys wear in olden days flapped around his legs. His dark hair brushed against his collar, and he had at least a day's worth of stubble. A worn hat was pulled low over his eyes, but what held her attention was the rifle in his hand.

Fear crept along her nerves as she got back into the car, locking the doors manually. The man continued to stride toward her. There was nothing she could do but wait. Who was he? And what was he doing out here so far from anywhere?

Her eyes were glued to him as he drew closer. She scooted away from the window, as if that would help, but when he tapped on the window she jumped, she was so nervous.

"Are you okay, ma'am?"

Don't miss TEXAS REBELS: EGAN by Linda Warren,
available April 2015 wherever
Harlequin® American Romance®
books and ebooks are sold.

www.Harlequin.com

Love the Harlequin book you just read?

Your opinion matters.

Review this book on your favorite book site, review site, blog or your own social media properties and share your opinion with other readers!

Be sure to connect with us at:
Harlequin.com/Newsletters
Facebook.com/HarlequinBooks
Twitter.com/HarlequinBooks

HARLEQUIN®

A *Romance* FOR EVERY MOOD™

JUST CAN'T GET ENOUGH?

Join our social communities
and talk to us online.

You will have access to the latest
news on upcoming titles and special
promotions, but most importantly,
you can talk to other fans about your
favorite Harlequin reads.

Harlequin.com/Community

Facebook.com/HarlequinBooks

Twitter.com/HarlequinBooks

Pinterest.com/HarlequinBooks

HARLEQUIN®

-A *Romance* FOR EVERY MOOD™

**Stay up-to-date on all your
romance-reading news with the
Harlequin Shopping Guide,
featuring bestselling authors, exciting new
miniseries, books to watch and more!**

The newest issue will be delivered right to you
with our compliments! There are 4 each year.

Signing up is easy.

EMAIL

ShoppingGuide@Harlequin.ca

WRITE TO US

HARLEQUIN BOOKS
Attention: Customer Service Department
P.O. Box 9057, Buffalo, NY 14269-9057

OR PHONE

1-800-873-8635 in the United States
1-888-343-9777 in Canada

Please allow 4-6 weeks for delivery of the first issue by mail.